DRAGON'S REDEMPTION

RED PLANET DRAGONS OF TAJSS BOOK 17

MIRANDA MARTIN

Copyright © 2020 by Miranda Martin

All rights reserved.

No part of this book may be reproduced in any form or by any electronic or mechanical means, including information storage and retrieval systems, without written permission from the author, except for the use of brief quotations in a book review.

❀ Created with Vellum

CONTENTS

Chapter 1	1
Chapter 2	10
Chapter 3	20
Chapter 4	25
Chapter 5	29
Chapter 6	39
Chapter 7	44
Chapter 8	48
Chapter 9	53
Chapter 10	57
Chapter 11	61
Chapter 12	68
Chapter 13	74
Chapter 14	80
Chapter 15	85
Chapter 16	94
Chapter 17	99
Chapter 18	108
Chapter 19	117
Chapter 20	129
Chapter 21	136
Chapter 22	143
Chapter 23	147
Chapter 24	159
Chapter 25	165
Chapter 26	169
Chapter 27	174
Chapter 28	180
About the Author	185
Also by Miranda Martin	187

1

DELILAH

"Could you chop these up for me, Nora?"

"Sure, got it!"

"Thanks." I smile, handing over the vegetables.

I appreciate the company and the help in the kitchen. At this point, Nora is a chef in her own right, but cooking is still my duty to the Tribe.

I grab a long-handled spoon to stir the huge pot of simmering stew. Dipping out some of the broth, I blow on the steaming liquid and take a careful sip. I close my eyes to enjoy the burst of flavor over my tongue.

Good, but a bit more of the salt-like mineral we discovered will make it better. I take a generous pinch from the jar on the work surface next to me and sprinkle it into the pot. A couple more herbs will brighten the flavor up too. I cut off some leaves from a woody stem, add a splash more water, and put the lid back on to let it do its thing.

"Almost done, Delilah," Nora calls out, the knife moving expertly in her hands, breaking down the vegetables in even little chunks that will cook fast.

There isn't that much time left until dinner. Even if there

was, I like to be efficient where I can—with the entire Tribe to feed, I'd be in the kitchen twenty-four seven if I dawdled.

"Great. When you're finished, just dump 'em in. I'm going to go grab a few more things from the garden," I reply.

"All right," she says.

She tosses me that sweet, shy smile that says so much about who she is. There's a reason the kids love her. There is no doubt she will be an amazing mother, I think, looking at her swollen belly.

"Nora! Nora!"

Speak of the little devils. I laugh as the kids rush in past me, surrounding Nora, their chubby little cheeks glowing from the heat and exertion, their delicate wings and horns only adding to their cherubic looks.

The twins Elneese and Ganeese are toddling after Zoe as usual.

"Hey, guys," Nora says with infinite patience as I head to the garden.

The sound of her voice makes me smile, but the expression fades as the garden comes into sight. Some of the girls are working, and their mates are with them.

Ryuth leans in and steals a kiss from his mate, a smile blooming on Mei's face in response. The romantic part of my heart flutters at the sight. Even after having twins—the very same ones now talking Nora's ear off, no doubt—they're completely connected. And they aren't the only ones.

Padraig whispers something to Maeve that makes her blush. Penelope kisses Bashir's cheek before he turns to leave. Little touches, little indicators that they're a couple. A unit, not alone. I sigh, seeing example after example of mated bliss.

It warms my heart, makes me hopeful for the future of the accidental society we've created—an odd mixture of Zmaj and humans, a collision of the destroyed past on this planet and the present. Hope is good. That future is what the gorgeous babies who are the result of the human and Zmaj matings will live in and that's all wonderful. But...

But.

Is it bad that I ache in my own heart watching everyone else with their partners? That there is a niggle of discontent at the sight of what they have? I'm happy for them, I really am. But I can't help but wonder.... What about me?

Am I destined to be alone while everyone else builds their families? While they look forward to a future surrounded by their children and even grandchildren?

"Delilah! Dinner smells amazing!" Mei says, smiling and straightening, hands on hips as she stretches out her back.

Everyone else chimes in their agreement.

"I can't wait to eat!" Maeve says.

"The thought of dinner is what keeps me going—so all of this productivity is thanks to you Delilah!" Penelope laughs.

I laugh as my cheeks warm, and a warm glow forms in my chest at the praise.

"Thanks guys—though if you never tell me when something is bad, I'll never change it," I warn.

Mei snorts, wiping sweat from her forehead with the sleeve of her shirt. She's not the only one sweating. I'm perpetually damp from the heat here on Tajss. The seasons are summer, summer, and oh yeah, more summer for some variety. A desert climate with everything that entails. Scorching heat, scarce water, more sand than you know what to do with. Good times.

"Nothing you make is ever bad—at worst, it's just good instead of amazing," Mei returns with a smile.

I shake my head, chuckling as I crouch down near the neat little patch of herbs. I know for a fact that's an outright lie. There's more than a couple of things I had to throw out before they ever made it to the dinner table. Experimenting with alien herbs and spices along with the meat and produce can lead to some interesting results.

Once, the pot literally started smoking from the combination of things I threw in it. I had to call in some reinforcements to help me upend that pot some distance from the cave system so that it wouldn't smoke everyone out, and my throat was raw from coughing for a couple of days.

I never repeated that particular experiment. Though on the scale of things that can go wrong, I'm never all that worried in the kitchen. Comparing it to my former job as an engineer, the stakes aren't the same.

On the ship, one mistake could result in a serious malfunction that could potentially hurt or kill people. So yeah. Tossing food together isn't all that high stress of a job in comparison. And I enjoy cooking for everyone too.

It reminds me of taking care of my younger brother and sister. With my father dead long before I could form a memory of him and mom drowning her grief in drink and men, it was up to me to take care of the kids that came from her high-risk behavior.

It sounds horrible, but it wasn't all bad. I loved them so much, loved making dinner for them, dressing them up in the cute clothes I managed to scrounge up despite our lack of money. I had no father, and my mother was absent at best, but I knew love. My brother and sister loved me and needed me, and that was enough.

An emptiness throbs in my chest, and I sigh. Sometimes, I can't believe that they're gone. One tiny portion of the massive casualties from the ship's crash.

They aren't getting a chance to live this life free of the confines of a ship. They don't have this opportunity to breath in fresh air instead of recycled, to look up and see sky. To look over the horizon and not be sure what's beyond the next rise. They would want me to make the most of this.

DRAGON'S REDEMPTION

I try to use their memory to snap out of it, but unfortunately the internal pep talk isn't doing a whole lot for me today.

I trim what I need off the thriving plants in front of me and throw the cuttings into the small basket I brought along. I wave goodbye to everyone still working and head back to the kitchen. As soon as I'm out of sight my shoulders drop.

Living in a communal situation like this, I pretend that I'm fine to avoid somebody asking what's wrong. What would I say?

We have food, water, shelter.

Sure, it's hot as hell on this planet, but we're in a much better situation than we were when we first crashed. I have people who care for me, as I care for them. We all work together. I have friends that I know will be there if I need them. They've already proven themselves. Still.

There's more to life than having physical needs met. Or even having friends. Right? No matter how I try to see the brighter side of everything, try to keep myself busy, there's something missing.

When I go to my pallet alone at night, that small splinter of a feeling rises to the surface. I've lost more than a few nights of sleep because of this empty feeling of being alone. I'm part of a community, part of something bigger than myself. A community that needs me, that I fit into and am most definitely a part of, but I don't have anyone who's mine. Someone who puts me as his priority. Who would be there for me in the middle of the night if I need to talk. Who would cuddle me when I turn over.

Admit it, Delilah. I'm jealous. I want my own Zmaj. I want to be treasured like Lana, Maeve, Penelope, any of the other girls. Unfortunately though, there are no more Zmaj to be had, so the entire point is moot.

"No Ell!" Ganeese yells, chasing his brother.

5

Ganeese leaps on Elneese as I walk in, and the two toddlers wrestle over the lid to a pot. Nora quickly separates them while Zoe watches, shaking her head. Zoe looks at me with a look that clearly indicates her thoughts. She shrugs and sighs dramatically.

"Enough," Nora says, picking up Elneese.

Ganeese leaps back to his feet and uses the pot lid as a shield, sword fighting with an imaginary opponent.

"Down!" Elneese shouts, wrestling against Nora's grasp until he slides down and drops towards the floor, his tiny wings fluttering madly to try and slow his descent.

I smile and set the basket down on one of the counter tops.

"Having fun?" I ask, winking at Zoe.

"Oh good—you're back!" Nora exclaims, setting down Elneese. "Do you mind watching them for a bit?"

"Sure, no problem," I respond right away, smiling at the kids.

They're so damn adorable, how could I say no? Nora hightails it out of the kitchen before I finish agreeing. I adjust the herb basket so I can watch them while I pick the leaves off.

"Can I help?" Zoe asks, looking up with big, hopeful eyes.

"Sure, sweetie. Here, just pick off the leaves like this," I say, showing her.

She watches intently as I show her what I want her to do. Poking out her bottom lip, her small fingers get to work.

"Good job," I praise, stirring the stew while I watch. "Just make sure you—"

A loud crash cuts off my thought and I jerk around to find the source. Elneese and Ganeese have pulled clean pots out of the storage shelves and are slamming them together on the dirty floor.

"Oh no!" I rush over. "No, guys, these are clean. Here, you

can bang these around," I offer, taking the clean ones and handing them ones that need to be cleaned anyway.

"Oops!" Zoe exclaims.

The herb basket is upended over the table scattering its contents.

"Sorry!" Zoe says, crestfallen.

"It's okay," I say, cleaning up the mess. "Accidents happen."

A thud is followed by an odd rolling sound behind me. This time, the twins have jars full of various ingredients and are rolling them across the ground.

"Woah guys!" I exclaim as one jar pops open, spilling its contents as I hustle over.

The twins stop and look up.

"Bad?" they ask in unison.

"Yes," I say, shaking my head. "This is food, we need to care for it."

"Oh," they say together, looking at the mess. "We help!"

Together they try to sweep the spilled contents back into the jar, taking the sand and all along with it. It's only a second before Elneese's hand blocks Ganeese, and they're on each other wrestling.

"Boys," Zoe sighs.

"Right?" I agree and she laughs.

Watching the boys wrestle causes a warmth in my chest, and after a moment's thought I decide to let them carry on. They're not hurting each other or anything else, and there are definitely worse things they could be into.

Zoe holds out her arms, so I lift her up onto the counter, and we work together picking the leaves off the stems, letting the boys wrestle and carry on as they want.

"This is fun," Zoe says.

"I'm glad you like it," I say.

"You need a boy, like mommy and daddy," she says, stopping and staring at me with her big eyes.

My heart hammers hard, and my mouth goes dry.

"You think?" I ask, trying to ignore the nerve she hit.

"Yes," she says, nodding. "You should have someone. You will be a good mommy. Someday I'll be a mommy too. I'm going to be the first mommy of my kind."

"Oh you are, are you?" I ask.

"Yes," she says matter of fact.

"What about Rverre? She's older than you," I point out.

"Bah!" she says, shaking her head. "She's going to be a warrior, like Lana."

"Lana has Aeros," I point out.

"But she was so slow in having a baby!" Zoe says, standing up and putting her hands on her hips. "I'm not waiting around. I'll be the best mommy ever!"

She's so serious I suppress my laughter. She's too cute and determined, but I don't want to hurt her feelings.

"I have no doubt you will be," I agree.

"Boys!" she yells at the twins.

The two of them stop rolling on the floor and look up at her. She holds up a tiny hand, pointing a finger at them.

"What?" they ask in unison.

"Be good!" she says, waggling that tiny finger.

The twins look at each other, and I see it coming too late. They leap into the air like a blur and tackle her as one. The three of them crash across the worktable knocking tools and dinner prep everywhere. The boys pin Zoe down and tickle her. She fights and laughs at the same time.

"Enough!" I raise my voice to cut through their din. They stop and look abashed. "We have to clean this up for dinner. Tonight is Aeros's birthday celebration! We don't want him to have a bad birthday, do we?"

"No, Delilah," the boys say.

"Right," I agree. "Now, help clean this up."

"Sure," they all agree and set to it.

They are helpful too, mostly. They're small and still getting control of their bodies but they do their best, and that's more than good enough for me. Once we're done and the stew is boiling in the pot, I shoo them all out of the kitchen space, which is really a sectioned off portion of the larger cave. They run off to play until dinner, while I stop inside the cavern's shadows and look out over the Tribe.

It's a good life. I cook, I clean, I contribute, as we all do. We're creating small comforts as time goes by. The wall that curves from the cliff wall out into the desert and back around to meet the cliff on the other side is done, solid and comforting as it keeps out most of the random creatures that would come exploring. The dome overhead protects us from the Invaders and hasn't been a problem for a while now.

The path that zig-zags its way up the cliff face has been widened and smoothed out, as have the crevasses where we each make our individual homes. We've even gotten almost-real doors, tanned leather stretched over metal frames salvaged from the shipwreck, but effective.

I sigh as I watch Samil kiss Inga, his face suffused with a softness that I never saw there before he found his treasure. The sight aggravates that seed of discontent inside me again, but I refuse to allow it to grow any more. Samil wasn't my type anyway. The sight of that kiss is only an unfortunate reminder that there aren't any eligible males left.

I turn away, shaking my head. What I have is enough. I'll have to make it be enough. And that's that.

2

DELILAH

"Delilah," Olivia's voice calls out from behind the tight leather door covering the entrance of my cave. "Can I come in?"

I jerk awake, startled from a deep sleep. It takes me a second to register what's happening as I sit up and rub the sleep from my eyes.

"Uh, sure," I reply.

She doesn't sound worried, so why is she waking me up early? The suns aren't shining through the door, so it has to be early. She opens the door and ducks inside, the first rays of the morning suns highlight the rich red of her hair. She's clearly already dressed to head out.

"Sorry to wake you up," she says, looking truly apologetic. "But Mei's supposed to come to the oasis with us today, and she's feeling sick. Any way you can fill in? Or do you have something else scheduled today?"

The oasis? Right, we need water and to gather whatever wood has fallen. I shake my head, to clear the sleep and throw off the thin covers.

DRAGON'S REDEMPTION

"No, I can come. Give me a minute to wake up and get dressed."

"Thanks Delilah! We'll wait for you by the wall—take your time," she smiles. She pauses at the door and glances back. "It's not fair, you know."

"Huh?" I ask, brow scrunching as I try to figure out what she's talking about.

"You," she says, shaking her head.

"What are you talking about?" I ask, hopping on one foot as I try to get my leg into my pants.

"I literally just now woke you up, and yet you look perfect," she says. "I'm jelly."

"Jelly? What?" I ask, unable to process the words she's saying into a coherent picture.

"Jealous, silly," she says.

"Uh, thanks?" I say, cheeks warming, but my leg finally gets into the pant like it should. Then I have to get the other one in.

I don't feel perfect. Heck, I'm feeling pretty proud I've gotten my pants on. Olivia smiles and shakes her head, then ducks back out through the curtain. I rub my face and run my fingers through my hair then straighten up my pallet.

A small group leaves the Tribe on a regular schedule to go forage for wood, seeds, berries, and anything else we can come across in the nearby oasis. Our garden is good, but there are things we just can't grow here.

We're lucky enough to have our own water source on site for necessities and to water the garden, but the conditions aren't right to grow some things, so foraging is a necessary chore. But man, is it early. Much earlier than I would usually get up, but getting an early start is a good idea.

An early departure time means the suns won't be beating down on us quite so hard during the trek. It will still be plenty uncomfortable, but there's no other way to do it.

MIRANDA MARTIN

Traveling at nighttime has its own set of problems. Coming across some of the deadly predators on this planet completely unawares, for one. The sismis, giant bat-like creatures that hunt in large swarms, only do so at night. A dozen other things that are more active during the cooler hours of night, all of them wanting to eat you. Yeah, it's not the best idea.

All right. Time to get moving. It's a new day, and I'm not going to indulge in any kind of self-pity. So I don't have a guy. Big deal.

I'm alive and healthy. That's a lot more than most of the people on our ship could say. I take my washcloth and spread it out on the bottom of my clay bowl. Grabbing my personal water container I carefully dampen it. Water is the most precious resource on Tajss. Nothing compares to its value. It is the stuff of life. Taking up the barely damp cloth, I use it to wipe off my face and wake myself up.

It doesn't matter that we have a water source, we live in the desert. Water is precious, and wasting it isn't prudent. I shove my feet into my shoes and grab my wide-brimmed hat. I'm darker than almost everyone here, so I'm not as prone to burning under the harsh suns, but a hat is still a good idea.

Dressed, I leave my cave and head to the kitchen to fill my waterskin and wrap up some jerky to take with me for the road. Shouldn't need more than that for such a short trip. We need to travel light so there is room in our packs to bring home everything we find.

Shouldering my pack, I walk over to the protective wall built around the cave system. It glistens in the sun, the meteor glass set in it sparkling beautifully. It gives everyone peace of mind to know we can protect ourselves with a literal force field. Myself included. Even the sight of the large wall and the reinforced metal gate is comforting.

When I reach the open gate, Ragnar, Olivia, and Ryuth

are already waiting. Originally, the group was supposed to be two couples—Ragnar and Olivia along with Ryuth and Mei. I suppress a sigh.

Sometimes I feel like my single status is forever being rubbed in my face. Probably because I'm raw about it so I give myself a mental slap. No self-pity! Not today, Satan!

"Morning," I call out.

Everyone turns and calls out greetings as I approach.

"Good. Let us begin our journey," Ragnar announces.

We murmur our agreement. We step through the gate in the wall and venture out into the vastness of the desert beyond. My feet sink into the soft, red sand. When our ship crash-landed on this planet, I remember waking up and taking in all the red. Red-streaked sky, red sand, red rocks.

For a moment, I thought maybe my vision was compromised, maybe I wasn't seeing the colors as they should be, but they'd stayed the same. It's all striations and variations on the single theme of red. Now, after years of living with this same view, I appreciate the harsh beauty of it. Even if another color or two would be nice.

Olivia steps over to Ragnar's side and he wraps a firm arm around her waist.

"Delilah?"

I look over at Ryuth's offered arm. Not surprisingly, humans aren't well adapted to the terrain here on Tajss. Our weight has us sinking into the hot sand with every step, slowing us down to an excruciating pace. Unlike the Zmaj.

Even though the dragon men are freaking seven feet of dense bone and pure muscle, with the addition of long reptilian tails, they don't sink into the sand because of another key adaptation.

Wings.

Not bird wings, with plumage and the whole fluffy shebang. No, their leathery, streamlined wings aren't meant to take actual flight. They help them leap longer distances, keeping them airborne for a longer period. Flaring the wings out helps them lift some of their weight off the ground, so they don't sink into the sand like we do. They glide across the soft, fine stuff like it's metal or concrete.

Unlike us humans, who sink in with every step, fighting the sand to make any kind of progress forward. Needless to say, they're a heck of a lot faster out here. And the faster the better with all the potential threats we could encounter.

"Thank you," I murmur, stepping into Ryuth's body and allowing him to wrap a secure arm around me.

And we're off. I grip his hard forearm, squinting against the air as he glides forward, next to Ragnar and Olivia.

"Is Mei all right?" I ask as we continue.

Ryuth glances down at me.

"She woke with a headache," he explains. "I told her not to come—the heat would only make it worse. She went back to sleep in the dark."

"Ah."

Sounds like she has a migraine.

"My thanks for coming in her place," he adds.

"No problem," I murmur sincerely. "We need to watch out for each other."

He nods, looking back up to continue scanning the rolling dunes around us, his eyes sharp. I've noticed that about the Zmaj, especially out here in the open. They never stop looking for potential threats. Not that I'm complaining. Who knows how many of us would have survived this long without the Zmaj to help us.

"How you doing over there?" Olivia calls out.

"Fine!" I return, glancing over. "Ryuth?"

"Good," Ryuth adds. "We are making good progress."

That's true.

"How much farther to the oasis?" I ask, adjusting my grip.

He looks around.

"We are perhaps halfway on our journey," he judges. "If we—"

"Ryuth," Ragnar interrupts, shifting closer to us. "We should veer this way and circle around."

He jerks his head to the left. Frowning, Ryuth looks. I see what Ragnar is gesturing towards at the same time Ryuth does. Deep footprints in the sand. The toes aren't distinct, indicating a more diffused pressure. The kind of prints you would get with webbed feet.

Guster. A chill flows through me.

"Good idea," Ryuth mutters, shifting course.

I ditto that sentiment. I have no desire to encounter those things. I'd be fine and dandy with never seeing one again in my life, thanks.

"I hope they aren't getting a drink at the oasis," Olivia comments, her head turned in the direction of those prints.

"Yeah," I agree, looking around with a sharper gaze now. "I hope they're gone."

The rest of the trip is tense after that sighting. Ragnar and Ryuth focus even more on our surroundings, talk quieting down so as not to inadvertently draw attention to our small party. I wait to see a menacing shape appear from the hazy red distance.

To say I'm on edge the rest of the way is an understatement. When the distinctive green of the oasis comes into view, I breathe a silent sigh of relief at the sight. We're not necessarily safe in the oasis, but at least we'll be halfway done with this trip.

With luck, there's nothing lying in wait that the guys can't handle. Then we can just grab what we need and head on back in time for dinner. I cross my fingers, hoping those thoughts didn't just jinx the rest of this trip.

This particular oasis isn't like the others I've encountered.

MIRANDA MARTIN

For one, it's huge, with an abundance of water. Hell, it has actual waterfalls. And it has the lush greenery that goes along with that.

In short, it looks gorgeous out here in the middle of all that dry desert. It looks perfect. Almost a fantasy come to life, but then you have to realize this is the one place that every animal for hundreds of miles comes to get a drink.

Oh, and it's Tajss, so even the plants will try to kill you. But we've survived many a trip to this place. I hold on to that knowledge as we near the edge of the tree line and Ragnar and Ryuth slow to a stop.

"Stay near us," Ryuth murmurs, watching the foliage.

Unlike the rest of the desert, this area is set apart by the massive trunks of the baoba trees and various plants and bushes, packing in tight around the source of water. It looks beautiful, but you can never forget. There are plants that paralyze, animals that can attack out of nowhere.

So, yeah. I'm going to be as careful as I can be. The Zmaj go first, Olivia and I follow closely after. I breathe a sigh of relief as we enter the shade of the trees. A hat can only do so much, after all.

The bushes rustle to the side, drawing my attention, and I freeze, heart in my throat. What is it? In the next instant a tiny shape scuttles away, clearly frightened. I let out a sigh of relief.

"That was way scarier than it should have been," Olivia mutters.

"Yeah," I agree, shaking my head.

Being away from the safety of the cave system definitely makes me paranoid. Maybe paranoid isn't the right word. Or, if nothing else, it's not a bad thing. If there are as many dangers as we know roaming out here, maybe paranoia is the proper response. Slowly we venture deeper into the oasis.

"Here," Ragnar whispers.

DRAGON'S REDEMPTION

No need to project our location to anything within hearing distance. I walk over along with the rest, noting the humidity in the air and the sound of rushing water nearby. It's tantalizing, but we have work to do.

We all gather around and see the fruit-laden bush he points to, the red berries ripe for the plucking. Perfect. Olivia and I set to work on them as the guys continue to explore, keeping us within calling distance.

Wiping off my brow, I reach for more water, but there's only a couple drops left. I look through a gap between the leaves to our right, seeing the distinctive sparkle of water. I clearly hear the sound of a waterfall.

"I'm going to go fill my waterskin," I tell Olivia, stepping back.

She glances over towards the water as well, nodding.

"All right. Be careful. And call out if you need help, okay?"

"Will do," I reassure her.

I wouldn't dare venture so far that they couldn't hear me call for help. She nods, turning back to the bush. I step onto the narrow, beaten path we've taken in thus far, trying not to think of all the animals that have come this exact way in order to keep a clear path, even of such a small size. It's fine.

When I break through that last bit of green, I stop on the sandy edge of the water, looking around for any obvious sign of danger. Apart from the sound of the water splashing into the sizable pond, it's quiet.

I don't see anything that sets off alarms. No obvious footprints, no rustling bushes, nothing that would indicate I should turn back. As satisfied as I can be, I turn my attention to the water. It reflects the sunlight streaming through the leaves. Rainbows dance in the air as water refracts the light. The rippling shine combines with the bubbles created by the small waterfall to obscure the depths of the water, but there's never been any fish or lizards under there. I'm not worried.

I know from experience the water here is safe to drink, clear and filtered through the ground like it is. I stare at the water longingly as I approach it, wishing I could strip and jump in. The sight of it makes me even more aware of my sweaty self. I can't just strip and jump in with Ragnar and Ryuth here.

Maybe after we're finished gathering everything we need, I can ask them if Olivia and I can jump in with our clothes on. They'll dry fast in this heat. And they could definitely do with a wash after traveling through the desert.

I crouch, open up the waterskin, and lean forward to scoop up some of that clear goodness. I should drink as much as I can while we're here and refill it before we head back to the Tribe. The water is cool against my fingers as I push the skin under the top, little bubbles floating to the surface.

I'll just keep it under until—

A large, tanned hand clamps down on my wrist.

A wet hand.

From under the water.

I suck in a tiny, precious gasp of air, but that's all I have time for before that hand yanks me under the water.

I let go of the waterskin, clawing at the tight grip of that hand, but it doesn't let go. I look at the surface of the water above me, the lights dancing on it as I'm spun around.

My back hits something hard, and what feels like an arm clamps down around my waist from behind.

I kick and twist, trying to break out of the hold. My heart pounds in my ears. Bubbles float to the top as I struggle. If I can just get to the top, I could call out for help.

I push and shove, trying to punch back, but the water takes the strength out of my blows. My clothes weigh me down even more, twisting around my body and making it harder to move.

My vision darkens around the edges. My lungs burn.

No!

I dig my fingernails into whoever or whatever is holding me, clawing for all I'm worth. It doesn't faze my captor. I keep my eyes on the bright light above as my limbs get heavier and heavier.

That edge of shadow in my vision grows. Or is the light above me dimming?

I don't...know...

Darkness surrounds me.

3

JORMUND

*T*reasure. My treasure.
  Mine.

I can't take my eyes off of her as the group she is with enters the oasis. I stopped for water, but this is so much more. My primary cock hardens, pulsing with need, responding to the fire deep in my soul. The dragon has laid its claim.

She is my treasure.

Carefully, I blend into the trees, waiting for an opportunity. There are two males and another female. Two is dangerous so I hold back and wait.

Watching.

She is exotic. Captivating. Female. A beautiful female. And she is *mine*.

I intended to avoid the group, seeing them long before they noticed me, but then I heard her voice. The sound of it wrapped around me and would not let go. It drew me in, pulling me closer to the group.

It was a siren song that forced me to follow it, and when I saw her... I knew.

The light shines on her dark skin and her fluffy hair, so unique, she is different than anyone I've seen. She doesn't have scales, her body is curvy, even her chest swells in a way that entices my imagination. Her full lips call, and I want to taste them.

Mine.

She is mine to protect. To care for. She is the one I'm destined for. My treasure. The one who will bring meaning and light to my life. I will keep her safe from every danger.

She and the other female, a larger one with lighter coloring and fiery hair, set to gathering berries from a bush. That one does not spark interest in me, for she is not the one my dragon wants.

I need *this* female.

I gaze at her perfect face, noting the long curling lashes, high cheekbones, plump lips. Her skin is perfection, gleaming with health under the sunlight. Working my way slowly closer I can now see her hair is a thick mass of tight curls a few shades darker than her skin. She looks even better this close than she did far away.

I must take her far from the others, far enough away that they cannot take her back. I must protect her. Mine. She is *mine*.

The dragon is patient. I am too. I watch the warriors with her and listen to their conversation. I can't understand their words. Some part of me knows I should. It's been so long since I've used words. The past is gone, a gray fog covering all but what matters. Now is all, yesterdays are gone.

Stay still. Wait. Observe. She is meant to be mine. My treasure. Fate will intervene. I need only wait.

The two males walk off, and I smile, nodding to myself. Opportunity presents itself.

As soon as they're out of sight, I slip from the brush of my hiding place and slide into the cool water of the oasis pool.

The sounds of the waterfall cover my movements. I duck under the water and swim across the pool before risking coming up for air.

I rise above the water just enough to take in air through my nostrils and see where my target is. She wipes her brow with her arm then says something to the other female. The language is strange, unfamiliar, and musical to my ears.

Anything she says would be music to me. It doesn't matter what language she uses. Her voice is an instrument singing the tunes of the stars. Soon it will be mine.

She moves, coming to the water, and I slide back beneath the surface. The suns are almost directly overhead and will obscure her vision. Perfect. Fate has made everything line up. This is my chance.

A waterskin breaks the surface, bubbles rising as it fills, but the smooth-skinned hand holding it is my signal. I grab her arm and pull her under in a single, swift motion, kicking us backwards as I do.

She struggles against me. Of course she does. She doesn't know yet that she is mine and I am hers. Something niggles at my thoughts, scratching, but I ignore it. The way she fights against me is of concern. I can't let the others figure out that I'm taking her with me. The other males will not want to give up their female, but she is not theirs.

She twists and turns in my arms and almost breaks free, but then she stops struggling, going limp. She'll need air fast, but I have to reach the far side of the pool before I can surface again. Pulling my wings tight against my body, I use my tail to increase my speed through the water, and in a moment we reach the opposite bank.

I surface, check the far shore, and find no one is looking for us yet. Good, I have time. I shift her limp weight in my arms, climb out of the water, and race into the jungle. Straining my ears for any sounds of pursuit or a cry of

DRAGON'S REDEMPTION

alarm, I run through the trees, dodging around the large trunks.

I keep glancing over my shoulder to make sure I'm not being followed. I skid to a stop barely outside the reach of a cvet. The beautiful plants spread their vines out wide, causing paralysis in anything unfortunate enough to land in their grasp. The plant then pulls in its prey and devours it slowly.

My hearts pound as my thoughts race. I have to get further away. I can't protect her and fight two males. I take my bearings quickly, then plot a path around the cvet that won't cost too much time. Two strides back, then I run and leap, dodging the plant.

It shivers when I land, rustling the foliage around it, but none of its vines whip out towards me. Crouching, I cover her with my body protectively and listen. The soft buzz of life in the oasis continues unbroken, accented by the sound of her soft breaths. No pursuit, no outcry, good.

The edge of the oasis is right here. We'll be exposed in the open as soon as I exit until I can put some distance behind us. This is the moment where our fate will be decided.

A strange sensation causes my scales to itch and tingle. My treasure shifts in my arms but remains unconscious. Time is not on my side. It's now or never.

A final glance over my shoulder, and then I burst from cover and run. Spreading my wings to lighten my weight, I bound forward, racing up the nearest dune. There is no help for the tracks I'm leaving behind, though.

The soft, warm breeze will erase them in time, but will there be enough?

It's a chance I have to take. I run as fast and as hard as I can, put as much space between us and their pursuit as possible. I growl under my breath as I slide down a dune, ensuring my body takes the entirety of the impact.

I must keep her safe. I travel for... a long time. I cannot stop, not when those other Zmaj may be following. My legs keep moving, my eyes keep watch for any danger coming. I have more than just myself to protect now. I must take care. She must never come to any harm.

Ever.

I will not allow it. She is in my care now. I travel through the day, pushing myself until the suns begin to dip in the sky. Until the light begins to wane. The dark is not a safe time to travel. And I have likely traveled far and fast enough to evade pursuit.

Adjusting course, I aim for a rocky cliff face with small caves embedded throughout. There is one in particular I like to use when traveling in this area. It should be suitable for the night. Climbing through the rocks with care, I find the small mouth of the cave.

I enter the shelter and sit down with my back against the wall, moving my female so she is cushioned on my lap, held against my chest. I stare at her, almost unbelieving of what I hold. My female. My treasure, but she is still not awake.

I am concerned about her still closed eyes. Setting my hand against her chest, I reassure myself that her odd heart-beat is still strong and steady. It is. Her delicate rib cage continues to expand and contract with her breaths. She is alive. But why is she still not waking?

I reach for my waterskin and carefully wet my hand. I wipe the damp palm across her forehead and the rest of her face, down the slim column of her neck, marveling at the softness of her skin. She frowns at the coolness, but she does not stir.

I sit her up, then make a loud noise, but that does not work either. Hmm. There must be some way to wake her....

4

DELILAH

*I*t's a struggle to open my eyes. Is it morning already? I don't even remember falling asleep....

Wait.

I dreamt about going to the oasis, and then the water was pulling me in. That can't be, so I must have fallen asleep at some point. Ugh, I feel like complete and utter shit. Blinking rapidly, I try to clear my blurry vision and clear the cobwebs from my head.

I shouldn't snack so close to bedtime. Wait. Is someone shaking me? Hold on. I'm not in my pallet. I'm not even lying down. I shake my head, my vision clearing abruptly, and stifle a yelp as I pull back a looming shadowy shape.

When I force my eyes to focus, the shape resolves into an unfamiliar Zmaj male who is staring at me. I let out an embarrassingly high-pitched scream, scrambling back as I realize I'm in his lap. What was I doing on his *lap*? He jerks his hands back. Large hands that a moment ago were cupping my shoulders and gently shaking me.

"Who the hell are you?!" I shout, my backwards momentum stopping as I hit a wall.

25

It's a cave. A strange, unfamiliar cave and it's small—I'm still only a couple of feet from him. My thoughts race, trying to make sense of what happened and how I got here.

"Hold on, hold on. Did you pull me into the water?" I glance around and there's a sad lack of anyone else in the vicinity. "Where are we? Where did you take me?"

There's an opening to my right, but I don't see anything familiar out there either. Then again, much of the desert looks the same to me. What is clear is that the suns are on their way to setting. It's almost dark. The last thing I remember is the suns being high in the sky, shining brightly down on that lovely water....

Right before this Zmaj pulled me in!

"This is kidnapping!" I cry out, turning back to him. He's still pushed up against the other side of the cave, his hands held up in a placating gesture. Really? "Why did you take me from my group? I need to get back right away! Do you hear?"

He frowns, his dark brows coming together over truly arresting eyes. I blink and only then register what he looks like. Like the rest of the males of his race that I've encountered here on Tajss, he's big. Huge would be a more appropriate way to describe him. Probably seven feet tall or so, much like the others.

And built. Broad shoulders, heavily muscled chest and abs, strong arms and legs. Easy to see because he's wearing one of those brief almost-loincloths that some of the Zmaj wear.

Dark, rich hair falls around a roughly carved, masculine face, partially obscuring the short horns I know are there. Strong jaw, high cheekbones, a nose with a bump along the bridge like perhaps it was broken at some point. But it's his eyes that really draw my attention.

They're a pretty lilac with a bright blue starburst pattern in the center, highlighted by thick, dark lashes and brows.

DRAGON'S REDEMPTION

They almost glow against the deep tan tone of the scales that line his body with bright blue tinting along the edges. The golden light of the setting suns shine in and catch the lavender shift of his eyes, making them sparkle.

His muscled tail shifts behind him, his leathery wings neatly folded as he stares with wide eyes. Why does he look startled? He's the one who took me!

"Who are you?" I push, shaking my head.

He frowns harder and grunts. Grunts! Like... like a gorilla! I scrub at my face, tamping down on my frustration.

"I need more than sounds, damn it!" I drop my hands to stare at him. "Where are we?" I repeat. "Why did you take me?"

He tilts his head to the side, clearly confused by the words and grunts some more. Like an animal rather than a thinking, sentient being. Shit shit shit.

He's clearly not in his right mind. I stop talking and wrap my arms around my middle. Okay. I take a deep breath. I need to think clearly here, even though what I want to do is scream and panic. Perhaps run around in a tight circle and tear my hair out, but that won't do me any good.

He hasn't hurt me. Well. Apart from almost drowning me there in the beginning. But I'm wondering if that was a clumsy mistake on his part.

He doesn't seem to be thinking on a higher level. Unless this is all some crazy, elaborate joke? I stare at his uncomprehending eyes. Nope. Don't think he's kidding. He's deep into the bijass, as the men call it.

Okay, what do I know? I look around, but it just looks like a cave. Glancing outside I take a more careful look at the area, but it doesn't look any more familiar. All right.

Assuming I could manage to escape this guy—which is a giant assumption, especially with him watching me as intently as he is right now—I have no idea where I am, and so no idea how to get back home.

That's a death wish out in that desert. I have no supplies, and even if I did, I don't know how long it would take me to stumble across something I can orient myself against. I would be out in the sun for a lot of that journey, prone to possible heat stroke and dehydration. All that before even considering the predators out there that I have no defense against.

Bottom line—I can't survive out here alone. It's the stark, undeniable reality of Tajss. Maybe I'll see an opportunity at some point...

No.

I will find an opportunity at some point to get back to the Tribe. I have to believe that. Why did I have to split up from the group? It's the first rule of any horror movie I ever saw on the ship—never go off alone! Am I the too-stupid-to-live cheerleader? Oh man.

This is so embarrassing. At least I had my shirt on. Ugh.

I look at the handsome Zmaj, his eyes focused on me, his body still. As if he's being careful not to startle me? I snort. Startling me is nothing compared to what he's already done.

"Well, asshole. Looks like you're stuck with me for now," I murmur, staring right back.

God help me, here I am. I'll make the best of it. At least he's good looking.

5

DELILAH

This night is not a comfortable one, and not just because there isn't anywhere soft to lay my head. I nod off propped against the hard rock, but keep jerking back awake when I remember I'm sharing space with a complete stranger.

One who can't talk, seemingly completely devolved into the bijass. The animalistic state the Zmaj fear, a kind of survival mode that can be triggered under too much stress. I don't know how old this Zmaj is—it's hard to tell with the Zmaj when their life spans are so long—but I'd guess he was around during the Devastation.

When the Zmaj society fell during the inter-planetary war over epis, the life-extending plant found only here on Tajss. If having everything you know crumble around you isn't enough to trigger a survival instinct, I don't know what is.

Plus, all the Zmaj females are gone, lost to sickness, or the Devastation itself from what I've gathered, so the chances of him being born post-Devastation are much slimmer. Impossible almost.

He hasn't hurt me so far, but I don't know what to expect from someone traumatized to the point that he's retreated into himself, leaving only the base instincts to drive the train. Not being able to communicate is the worst. I ponder over that fact, keeping a wary eye on his prone figure.

At some point, exhaustion gets the best of me, and I fall into a fitful sleep. I don't know how long I'm out but the light of day streams into the cave, waking me up. I jerk upright from my slumped position, nerves jangling with panic.

I'm hyper-alert and jittery, but immediately slow, wincing at the crick in my neck. Not a surprise, considering the sleeping conditions. The Zmaj is already up and by the mouth of the cave, looking out.

He turns when he hears me and points outside, grunting. I stare, not comprehending. He grunts again. Obviously, he wants me to go out there.

"Sure, why the hell not," I mutter, climbing to my feet. "Me Tarzan, you Jane. Maybe I should start grunting too."

I stop a conservative yard away. He eyes me, clearly curious, before offering a waterskin. The sight of it underscores exactly how parched I am. Saying no to water is not a good idea, no matter what the circumstances.

"Thank you," I murmur, taking the skin.

It's nice and full. Probably from when he was lying in wait under the water, waiting to strike. I sigh, tipping the skin back and taking a few careful sips. I wish I had my own waterskin with me, but apparently it didn't survive my abduction. I offer his skin back and he takes it, securing it at his hip once more.

Watching me, he steps out onto the shallow lip outside the cave. He points to the spot next to him, looking at me expectantly.

"Just call me Lassie," I mutter, stepping to that spot. "Now what?" I ask, knowing I may as well be speaking to nobody.

DRAGON'S REDEMPTION

Or making nonsensical sounds. Without warning, he slides an arm under my knees and behind my back, lifting me up against his chest. I gasp, clutching at his hard shoulders like a complete ninny. He freezes, watching me. Waiting to see if I'll freak and claw his eyes out, maybe.

"Don't worry," I mutter, looking away. "I know where my bread is currently buttered. Let's get out of here."

He must take his cue from the relative calmness of my voice. His wings flare out, and he leaps from the shelf and out across the rocks. I gasp as my stomach drops, and I tighten my grip around his neck. Not that his hold isn't plenty secure. I don't know if I could get out of it if I tried. The thought sends a bolt of unease through me. I shouldn't forget that fact. He's a lot stronger than me. He can do whatever he wants to do in the end. I shiver, trying not to freak myself out. There's no point.

We land softly in the sand. From then on, we're skimming across the dunes, fast enough that my hair blows back and I squint against the blown debris. You know what would be nice? My freaking hat. That's gone just like my waterskin. Probably floating uselessly in that pond. Or trampled under a waterfall.

Sighing, I lean my head against his chest. Might as well be comfortable. I don't know how far he plans on going today, and my neck is stiff from that terrible night's rest. He's taking me further from the Tribe, but it isn't like I have a lot of options. Or any control at all over where we're going.

So I stay quiescent in his arms, not knowing what else to do. Feeling helpless is not at all comfortable or easy. I try to keep my spirits up by imagining how I'll store up rations when he isn't looking. Bide my time, wait until he thinks I'm not even thinking of going anywhere. Then I'll make a break for it as soon as he leaves me alone for a moment, confident that I have no desire to run.

MIRANDA MARTIN

Maybe it's a fantasy, but I'll take whatever I can get. I glance at my kidnapper. There's not much else to look at. I keep track of landmarks we pass, but there aren't a whole lot of them. Besides, he's actually very attractive. It's a shame that he's, you know, completely off his rocker. That's just my luck.

Here's a virile, apparently unattached male. But, oh yeah, he's also crazy. I look away, back out over the expanse of the vast desert spread out in front of us. Better to keep my attention safely there. Thankfully, I don't have the whole day to spiral, lost in the maze of my own thoughts.

The suns are still bright in the sky when he veers towards another rocky section, this one larger than the one we stopped at. I take note of everything. Any of it might be useful later.

He takes us up a clear path to a larger hole in the cliff. I'm guessing this must be where he lives.

He steps inside and carefully sets me down on my feet. I wobble a little, unsteady after being carried for so long. He lets go only when it's clear I'm not going to fall over. I blink, waiting for my eyes to adjust to the relative darkness inside. I don't really have clear expectations, but whatever I was unthinkingly expecting, it isn't what I find.

The cave is a good size, not too big or too small. Comfortable. The floor is sandy and dusty, but solid rock. I look around—there's almost nothing in here. A pile of furs shoved in the corner. His blankets, I assume. I look around some more, like maybe I'm missing another section of it.

Perhaps a built-in set of cabinets and a working kitchen? But there's nothing else. My heart drops a little at the meager lodging. I bite my lip, looking over at the big Zmaj. He's watching. Waiting for my reaction?

I try a smile, even as my heart aches for this strong, handsome man who's been reduced to this. He's living like an

DRAGON'S REDEMPTION

animal. This is a hole in a cliff with some blankets. That's literally it.

Nobody should live like this. It's a clear indicator of the state of his life. No comforts, no softness. He's completely alone. Just surviving. I shouldn't feel for him. Really, I shouldn't.

He's my kidnapper, for God's sake! He almost drowned me and then forcibly took me away from my people. I know all that. But...

I look away from him and back at the cave. I can't deny the effect it's having on me. Maybe too much, but there you go. This... this damn near breaks my heart.

"Okay," I say out loud, stepping farther in. "Well I am going to go home. You're not keeping me here forever." I glance back to see his attention still on me. "But maybe we can make this a little more comfortable while I'm here."

What else should I do? I don't want to be away from all my friends and family. I will get back to them, somehow, but no matter what, he doesn't deserve to live like this.

"You've clearly never cleaned this place," I comment.

There is debris lying around mixed with the dirt, and that seems as good a place to start as any. I grunt as I try to pick up a particularly heavy rock. Large hands pluck it from me, and the silent Zmaj carries it out of the cave without a word. Or a grunt. I blink at his broad back. Well. He's not stupid.

"All right. Thank you," I say as he comes back in.

I get back to work. He takes care of the large, heavier rocks, and I move out the smaller ones. Now it's all dust and sand. How do I manage this?

I poke around the pile of stuff by his blankets and uncover some sticks and rushes. I tie them together to make the world's worst broom, but it gets most of the dust and sand out. I pick up the furs and carry them out of the cave. My large shadow follows.

MIRANDA MARTIN

Holding up the two corners, I hold one out to him and wait. He stares, a hesitant confused look on his face, then at last, he takes the corner. I punch the furs, and the force of it jerks his corner out of his hands at the same time a burst of dust and small gnat-like things fills the air. Coughing, I wave a hand in front of my face.

Frowning, I pick up the corner and hand it back to him. He takes it, staring at me, then the fur in his hand. His head tilts to one side and he grunts.

"Right," I shake my head. "Hold it tighter this time."

I punch it again and this time he holds his end tight. More dust and grotesqueness fill the air.

"Yeah, that's not sanitary," I point out, punching some more.

He watches me, a smile tugging at his lips as he stands there, waiting for me to finish.

"You think this is funny?" Punch, punch. "Maybe if you cleaned this place, I don't know, once a year even, I wouldn't have to do this!"

Eventually, the bursts of dust stop appearing and I gesture for him to carry them back inside. I follow him and he drops them back into the corner. Shaking my head I step past him and kneel on the ground, I arrange them neatly.

"See? Much better."

He stares at the furs and then back at me. No discernible reaction. I sigh, standing.

"A thank you would be nice, you know."

My stomach chooses that moment to growl. He looks from my stomach back to my face, taking a step back towards the opening of the cave. He gestures for me to follow.

"I was never great at Charades," I mutter, following him out.

Because, again—what else am I going to do? Hang out in

DRAGON'S REDEMPTION

the empty cave twiddling my thumbs? He turns to the left, reaching back to take his lochaber off the strap he has crossed along the middle of his back. The sunlight glints along the sharp edge. For some reason, that glint brings home the fact that he's dangerous much more than anything else has so far.

Which is really idiotic. I've seen firsthand the kind of damage Zmaj warriors can do with their massive bodies.

"Where are we going?" I ask, trying to fill the silence. Trying to use the sound of my own voice to calm myself really. He turns back around to me and slowly places his hand across his mouth. Quiet. Got it.

I follow along a couple paces behind him as he enters another cave, this one longer and deeper than the one we were in. I can't see the back of it. Shivering, I close the distance between us, staying closer to his back. Between him and whatever else could be in here, I'll take him. At least he's demonstrated he doesn't want to kill me, right?

Not yet, anyway. All the Zmaj I know would never hurt a woman, but... well, you never know. This one seems pretty gone. Almost worse than Ryuth before Mei came into his life.

He goes a few feet in and grabs a stick. Holding it in front of his mouth, he belches fire and voila we have a torch. We walk deeper into the cave, turning right as it does. I'm starting to think this is less a single cave and more a full network of tunnels. When it branches at one point, I know I'm right. We take the right tunnel.

The only sound is coming from my shallow breaths and the scuff of my feet. If I couldn't see, I would think that I was walking alone in here. We walk for a bit, through another branch and various natural rock formations, until I hear a small rustling sound towards the left.

The warrior's head swivels over there, and he reaches an arm back, his palm out in a 'stop' gesture. I freeze in place.

MIRANDA MARTIN

What made the sound?

He glides to the left, his lochaber silently swinging around in his hands. He moves like a jungle cat, smooth and silent. Stalking prey. Four steps. Five. Then he *moves*.

Leaping forward, he stabs the deadly blade behind a medium sized rock. I hear a small screeching sound. Though maybe that's the sound of the blade meeting the rock? Whatever it is, it makes me step closer to my escort.

The echo of the high-pitched sound feels like it could draw anything in the area upon our heads. Probably I'm just being paranoid. Probably.

The Zmaj bends over and pulls something off his blade. When he turns around, he's holding a round, furry creature with big eyes already glazed over in death. Gretba. I hug myself.

Meat is necessary, but it is a little harder to stomach the creature that's dying for my meal when it's kinda cute. Survival is hard here.

The Zmaj crouches and sets down his lochaber in favor of a large hunting knife he has strapped on the opposite hip from his waterskin. He gets to work skinning the plump creature, his hands moving deftly. This clearly isn't his first rodeo. At this point, it isn't mine either.

In no time flat, he has the thing skinned and dressed, ready to be cooked. And he barely got any blood on him. Impressive. Standing with the fruit of the hunt in his hand, he gestures for me to follow him back out. No need to tell me twice.

I'm happy to get out of there. The trip back out is a lot shorter, probably because we're not trying to be stealthy. Not that I'm all that stealthy in comparison. We all have our strengths.

When we reach the mouth of his home cave, he stops and

DRAGON'S REDEMPTION

reaches for some of the wood stacked against the outside. Huh. I didn't notice that before.

He uses one of the thinner pieces to skewer the carcass but gathers more in his other hand. Inside, a few paces over to the right, he stops near a charred stone circle obviously meant for cooking. After dumping the wood into the shallow pit, he takes a deep breath.

And then he blows a strong, orange-yellow stream of fire out from his mouth, igniting all the wood instantly.

A whooshing sound accompanies the quick burn, adding a dramatic flair to the whole thing. I make a small squeak, taking a step back from the rush of heat. I know the Zmaj can blow out fire due to the gland at the back of their throats that can release a flammable substance on cue. It ignites on contact with oxygen. Sort of like the fantasy dragons! Still, some warning would be nice.

"Maybe a heads-up next time, huh?" I say.

He glances at me before returning to fiddling with the skewer. Real convenient that he can't understand anything I say. Hell, I'm speaking his language even. He sets the meat up so it's high enough over the flame that it will cook evenly and not blacken instantly. I sit down on the ground, propping my head in my hands.

"Maybe I should fill in your end of the conversation myself," I mutter, watching the meat cook.

For a plain slab of meat without any seasoning at all, it smells pretty darned good. Of course, that might be because I'm ravenous. I stare at the sizzling meat as it cooks, feeling the gravity of the situation hit me.

I've been kidnapped by a nonverbal Zmaj warrior with no feasible way out of the situation. I'm isolated, without supplies or any idea where I am. There may not be a good time for me to make a run for it for quite a while.

Despair keeps trying to rise along with an overwhelming

feeling of helplessness. Is this some kind of cosmic punishment for not being happy with what I had? Am I trapped here? Am I going to die here?

A flat rock with a cooked piece of meat on it lands in front of me. I look up, taking the offering without thinking.

"Thank you," I murmur, watching him cut another piece for himself.

He gave me food first. That's... sweet. Damn it. I take a bite of the meat, humming at the taste of it. Some salt would be great, but I'll take it. Gratitude suffuses me as I fill my belly. I look at the Zmaj.

He's eating quickly, his eyes scanning the area around us. Keeping us safe. At this point I don't know what to think. Pity for him, gratitude for him taking care of me, anger at not having a choice, fear of what he might want, of what the future could bring.

There's so many things going on, I can't quite get a handle on how I feel. Maybe a good night's sleep will—

The ground lurches, and I'm thrown towards the crackling flames of the fire. I squeeze my eyes shut, bracing for the pain. There's no way to stop—

The air rushes out of my lungs as his hard arm catches me in my midsection, stopping me from falling in. I gasp in air, falling back as the earthquake keeps going, rocks slamming into each other, dust falling down from the cliff face behind us.

My fingers dig into the ground for purchase, but there's only a thin layer of sand and dirt covering the rock. There's nothing to hold on to…

6

DELILAH

he Zmaj growls as he rises to his feet. His eyes are narrowed and intense, his head whipping towards me. Cold ice balls in my belly, but there's nowhere to run. The ground is still shaking. Moving in a blur, he grabs me, strong arms wrapping around my much smaller body and cradling me against his torso. He rushes into the cave, lurching from side to side as he runs with the shaking underneath us.

When we reach the far corner of the cave, he shields me with his body. Dust falls from the ceiling as he crouches above me, but no debris reaches me. This isn't what I expected to happen from the expression on his face.

Staring at his admittedly sexy face, I try to decipher what he's thinking. I'm surprised at how quickly he was able to move us inside. The ground rumbles and bucks even here in the cave, though it's not as pronounced. It's better than being near the edge of the cliff, where the path drops off sharply. We'd have fallen for sure, but I wasn't thinking clearly enough to come to that conclusion, let alone do something about it fast enough.

39

His jaw clenches, lips tighten, he isn't as composed as his actions would suggest. The tension is easy to read on his face but there's more to this than that. Fear? Anger? Anticipation? I don't know.

"What's happening—"

I don't get to finish my question because his large, calloused hand covers my mouth. He shakes his head at me emphatically, snarling softly. I snap my mouth shut, eyes widening in response. No talking. Got it. No problem.

When I don't try to keep talking, he drops his hand, looking back to the cave entrance. It hits me. He's scared. Scared and angry, though that second emotion might be caused by the first. I don't understand. Yes, an earthquake is scary. I'm not arguing that, but this seems overboard for the situation.

Unless I'm missing something? Thankfully, the quake doesn't continue much longer, the shaking lessening and then finally stopping. He waits for a few beats once the ground is stable and then steps away, stalking out of the cave without any indication of where he's going or what he's doing.

Though how would he communicate it anyway? Smoke signal? Morse code? I look at the empty mouth of the cave, taking a few deep breaths until my heart stops racing. I've never felt an earthquake like that before. It wasn't just strong, it was long. Did they feel it in the Tribe's cave system?

Bracing a hand against the rock, I get shakily to my feet. The ground has stopped moving, but I'm still vibrating. All right, okay. I'm fine. A little sweaty and not completely steady, but fine.

And yeah, the Zmaj's reaction was kind of scary...but he didn't hurt me, even though he was clearly hanging on to himself by his fingernails. Was he only scared? Where did he

DRAGON'S REDEMPTION

rush off to? Did he just run in a panic and leave me here alone?

I debate what I should do. He doesn't come back in and outside is dangerous, so I shake my head, grab the makeshift broom and set to work. I need to get busy doing something, or my thoughts will get more anxious and scared. I set to work cleaning up the new film of dust and pebbles that broke off from the walls and ceiling of the cave.

Nothing big enough to be dangerous, luckily. Just irritating. I just cleaned the place! I glance over at the opening of the cave periodically as I work, but he doesn't reappear. When I finish sweeping and the place is as close to clean as I can make it, I move on to the banked fire outside.

Still no Zmaj males. I look out over the dark expanse of the desert, lit by gentle starlight. Am I wasting time right now? Should I be trying to make my way back to the City while I can? While I have this window of opportunity?

Carefully I look around, trying to get a handle on our location in relationship to the portion of Tajss I'm familiar with, the part I call home. I still don't see anything I can use to orient myself. If I've been near here before, I don't remember it. I take stock again.

Okay, if I leave now, I have no idea where I'm going. I'm almost certainly screwed if I have to survive alone out there in the desert. I can't hunt. I don't know where the nearest source of water is. I could only move through that sand at a snail's pace. For better or worse, I'm tied to my kidnapper. For now.

The very same conclusion I'd already come to. I sigh and finish cleaning everything I can clean. There isn't much to tidy, what with his, let's call it his minimalistic style of decorating. When I'm finished, I sit down on the furs, the only place with any kind of cushioning.

And then I wait.

MIRANDA MARTIN

And wait some more.

At a certain point, I decide lying down and waiting is just as effective, so I do that. There's no chance of me falling asleep though. I feel very alone in this dark cave, without even a weapon to defend myself.

Silence reigns as I listen to the sound of my own breathing. I jerk as something whistles but when I look for the source it turns out to be the wind. Something chirps and I jump again, only to find it was a small bug. Everything is louder in the silence. Even my own breathing and heartbeat sound loud.

Then I hear the footsteps. I sit up, hoping it isn't something else. Sitting up my heart races as I stare at the opening, anticipation winding tight. The dark shadow that steps into it is very clearly Zmaj shaped and I let out a sigh of relief.

He walks towards me and I hold my breath. The soft light from outside highlights the contours of his face, showing his calmer expression, but the set of his shoulders and his sharp eyes show that he's on alert, still wary.

He bends towards me and I tense. He grabs the fur nearest the wall, the one that I'm not using.

"Where did you go?" I ask as he straightens. He glances at me but doesn't try to answer as he turns and walks back to the cave entrance. Dismissively. "What was that earthquake?" I try again, watching him settle the fur down near the entrance. "Why were you so freaked out by it?"

He doesn't know the words, but the question in them has to be clear, right? He doesn't answer, settling down with his back towards me. Between me and the only exit. To block my escape? Or to protect me?

I lay down, considering his large, prone figure. Maybe both? I sigh, frustration burning hot. He's not going to communicate with me. Might as well try to get some rest

DRAGON'S REDEMPTION

while I can. I don't want to be tired if a real opportunity presents itself.

I close my eyes, expecting to have trouble drifting off, given the situation, but I don't.

Maybe my subconscious registers the fact that the Zmaj won't let anything happen to me. Or maybe I'm just too exhausted to stay awake. Either way, I welcome the soft embrace of sleep, burying my face in the fur underneath me as it envelopes me.

7

DELILAH

I startle awake. Something is wrong. I had a really bad dream. There was a strange Zmaj, water, an earthquake.

When I crack my eyes open to stare at the blank stone wall, it hits home. This isn't a dream. Damn it. A lot happened. None of it good, but that isn't all that's wrong. My body doesn't feel quite right.

I sit up. It's harder than it should be. I'm trembling slightly, and my joints ache badly. The kind of all-encompassing generalized pain a fever causes.

I know what this is. I was expecting it, though I was keeping my fingers crossed that it would take longer to hit. Epis withdrawal. Epis is a plant unique to Tajss that we eat, and it adapts our bodies somehow and helps us to survive in this harsh climate. It comes with a price. It's addicting. Very addicting.

Not just in a 'withdrawals will be really difficult but you'll get through it' way. No. If I don't get my epis dose soon, it's over. Lights out for good. Shit.

I take a deep breath, trying to push away the sensations.

DRAGON'S REDEMPTION

It's morning. The daylight is already strong, streaming in through the cave's mouth. The empty cave's mouth. I look at the unoccupied fur in front of it. No Zmaj in sight. Not noticing until then is a testament to how off I'm feeling.

Well. Now what?

I force my body to listen and rise up, using the wall for support. Standing doesn't improve my situation, but it doesn't make it worse. Great. I walk outside to see if he's nearby, feeling a little like an old lady as the aches and pains make themselves known. All I see when I get outside is the remnants of last night's fire and the red rock and desert. There's no sign of him in any direction.

All right. If I had to guess, I would say he probably left to hunt, but how long will he be gone this time? I've seen the Tribe's hunting parties go out. Sometimes it takes hours for them to return. Sometimes days. So, basically, I have no real idea how long he'll be gone. I could be well past withdrawals by the time he gets back, and not because I'm all better.

Shaking my head, I go back into the cave, empty and alone. Being solo on Tajss isn't safe, even if I wasn't also getting sick. What kind of kidnapper leaves the kidnapped alone and free this much? I shake my head sighing. Wishing for a more professional kidnapper has to be a new low.

I pace the perimeter of the cave, but there really isn't anything to see in here. Rock walls, ceiling, floor. Couple of furs. That's it. Uninteresting is a kind way to put it. I sit for a few minutes, then I walk around some more. Bored again, I lie down.

I repeat this cycle, over and over, until the small confines of the cave seem to be closing in. I'm not particularly claustrophobic, but I'm only human. And being in this cave is driving me bonkers. I've no doubt that not feeling great isn't helping either.

Knowing it's not the most prudent or safest thing to do, I

wander out of the minimal protection of the cave but once I'm outside, I hesitate. Behind me is safety, or as close to it as I'm going to have away from the Tribe. Out here is space, a degree of sanity, and the potential of hope. I can't wander too far, or I might get lost, lose my way back.

But space! Scenery! Change, any change, because at this point I'm going nuts. I have to exercise, at least attempt to walk off the pain. I should be okay if I keep the cave in sight, though. All right, it's a plan then. I walk down the path we took up to the cave. It's lined with rocks, and it's actually an easy straight shot down to the desert sand.

When I reach the bottom, my feet sink into the sand. I have no idea where to go from here, so I pick a random direction. As one does. Four steps in, I remember exactly why I hate traveling in the desert without a Zmaj escort.

My feet sink into the hot sand with every step, forcing me to fight for each step forward. I'm already feeling weak and everything hurts. This isn't helping in the slightest. Hmm.

Okay, this wasn't the smartest move I've made. I stop to take stock. When I turn around, I can clearly see the mouth of the cave. Turning forward again, I assess the situation. I'm halfway up a dune.

Maybe I'll just get to the top to get a better vantage point so I can look around, maybe find my erstwhile kidnapper. Better to know where he is. He hasn't really hurt me so far, but he's still a big fat question mark.

"Stupid sand," I mutter as I almost swim through it towards the top of the rise.

Hot sunlight, hot sand, hot air. Everything is hot. Stupid hot. Yeah, I'm definitely going back to the relative cool of the cave after I get to the top. Finally, I make it to the peak.

I sigh, lifting my head up from the sand so I can get a good look at the hard-won view. I immediately freeze when I see what's waiting for me on the other side of the dune.

DRAGON'S REDEMPTION

Guster.

A whole pack of them. My eyes dart, quickly counting. Five in total. I stare at the reptilian carnivores, apex predators here on Tajss, if you don't count the burrowing sandworm zemlja. Guster are huge, with hulking mounds across their backs, their bodies covered in thick leathery skin punctuated with sharp spikes scattered throughout to deter other predators from attacking. Not that they're prone to being attacked. To my knowledge, only zemlja are a real threat to them.

I watch with my heart in my throat as they mill about, their wide, webbed feet ensuring they don't sink into the sand like I do. One of them opens its mouth to emit that odd, howl of a dog blended with the hiss of a cat when another of its pack ventures too close. I stare transfixed at the razor-sharp teeth in that mouth. Icy tendrils flow out of my core and down my limbs as I realize just how screwed I am. If they see me, that's it. I'm toast. Okay, okay.

I have to creep back down the dune. Quietly. I keep my eye on them and step backwards. I let my foot slide down. The soft sand cushions any sound. I can do this. Slow and steady...

One of them lifts its head high, its nostrils flaring and contracting. My stomach clenches tight as the guster sniffs the air. Shit. My muscles are so tense they shake. I clamp my mouth shut to keep from making some stupid sound.

Slowly, it turns its head towards me. Slowly, its cold eyes pin me in place.

8

JORMUND

I slice into another section of the bivo with my hunting knife. It took me longer to track and hunt it down than I planned. I do not like leaving my treasure alone for this long, but I also want to ensure she has food to eat. A little more skin to take off the meat, and then I can return to—

A high-pitched scream rends the air, and I freeze, every muscle tensing. A feminine scream. Adrenaline shoots through my body as I leap to my feet and run towards the sound before I think it through.

My treasure. I know it is her. I will not let anything happen to her. I spread my wings and bound across the desert, faster than I can ever remember moving. A dim memory struggles to rise in the back of my mind.

Screams.

Masculine ones. Rushing to... do... something.

I shake my head, images and feelings and pain from the past swirling inside me. It is not clear, just as it has not been for... I do not know how long. It doesn't matter. What I do

DRAGON'S REDEMPTION

know is that it is not important in this moment. Only finding and protecting my treasure is.

I use the fear, the despair, the deep sense of loss, to push forward, to squeeze every bit of speed I can from my body. I cannot lose my treasure. I cannot!

I will not fail her.

Gritting my teeth, I leap over one last dune. The last one between me and my target. Time slows to a crawl. Each piece of what I see is a frozen tableau laid out before me. Information, coming in, processing. It happens in less than a beat of my hearts.

My treasure, sliding down a dune, fear in her eyes.

A pack of guster cresting that same dune directly behind her. Hunting her. Hunting my treasure.

Rage colors my vision red as I swing my lochaber up. The distance between us is too much. It seems impossible for me to reach her before they do. I have to save her.

Muscles coiling, knees bending, I leap up and forward, directing my leap towards the guster at the rear of the pack. I can't reach the one closest to *She-Who-Is-Mine*. My hope is to gather their attention from her.

I land solidly on its back, and its spine bows under the impact. The spiny protrusions slide across my own protective scales, causing only minor discomfort. Its howl screeches its displeasure.

I stab down with all my might, aiming my lochaber for the base of the beast's skull. The blade breaks through with a hard crunch, the tip sliding inside the softness beneath. The screeching turns into an odd warbling as the animal starts to buck underneath me, trying to dislodge the source of the pain.

The lochaber comes free with a squelching sound, coated in blood. I leap off the dying beast, straight towards the next-closest guster. It turns, seeing me coming.

It tilts its head back, jaws yawning open, displaying the rows of sharp teeth. Twisting my body, I change my trajectory and aim for the open patch of land to its right.

I hit the sand hard and roll to avoid its slashing mouth, feeling the gust of its hot, fetid breath upon my back. I turn to attack when I hear my female scream again.

Snarling, I abandon that guster and leap towards the sound. She is on her backside, scrambling back from a guster that is only a few arm spans away.

Too close. No time!

I roar as I land next to it, trying to draw its attention away from its prey. It whirls towards me, its already-open mouth darting out and snapping close.

I shift to avoid the bite, but only manage to avoid the animal clamping down on my torso. The teeth sink deeply into my arm instead. Clenching my jaw at the pain, I abandon my lochaber and reach for my hunting knife.

It shakes me in its mouth, and the pain is excruciating, but I block it out. Pain is a distraction I cannot afford. If this guster defeats me, my treasure will be left vulnerable.

That cannot be.

I wait for it to pause its frantic head shaking, deliberately going limp in its grip while feeling my blood drip down my body in a hot cascade. It hesitates, ceasing its powerful shakes when it does not feel me thrashing.

Now.

Pulling my arm back, I look it in the eye and stab it directly through that orb, my knife piercing past it. It drops me, rearing back with a howling screech. More blood gushes out from my wounds and the pain flashes hotter.

The guster turns and runs. It slams into one of its pack mates, entangling the two of them. They snap and hiss at each other, struggling to separate. Another of the guster is

DRAGON'S REDEMPTION

tearing at the meat of the slain. The two stumble over it, pulling its attention from its meal.

Those three snap and hiss at each other. The alpha of the pack eyes me with cold, calculating eyes. Guster are not intelligent, really, but they are cunning. The biggest of the beasts steps from side to side, shifting its weight. Its thick, leathery lips pull back, making it appear to grin.

I crouch and lean forward, not giving ground, raising my tail up behind me and spreading my wings. I growl, ready for it to attack.

It hisses, mouth opening enough to bare its teeth and for me to see its soft pink tongue flickering. I take a step forward, meeting its cold gaze. It steps back and I growl louder. Its head dips down as if to charge, but then it turns away. It emits a mewling sound, then breaks into a run. The rest of the pack stops, glances in my direction, then runs after their alpha.

I've succeeded in convincing the pack that this prey is not worth the price. It would not have worked had they been truly hungry. I watch the pack run, hearing their stampeding footsteps draw farther and farther away as they leave my line of sight.

Blood drips down my arms, but I ignore it until I'm sure they're not going to change their mind. When I look down, there is a puddle of deep red mixing with the sand. Too much of it, but I can wait a little more. I turn to my treasure, quickly scanning her body. Her normally rich skin appears ashen, her eyes wide with fear, but there is no sign of her being physically hurt.

I step towards her and stumble. My balance is not what it should be. Too much blood lost. Steeling myself, I close the distance between us, reaching out to her with my good arm. She does not fight when I take hold of her hand and pull her towards the relative safety of the cavern.

The path up to it has never felt so long.

9

DELILAH

I walk with the Zmaj back to the cave, wishing I was strong enough to carry him up the entire way. He's bleeding heavily from his torn up left arm, the blood leaving a trail as we walk. I have no idea how he managed to scare away a whole herd of those things—but he did.

He was like a one-man whirlwind, moving so quickly I had a hard time following his movements at every point. For a few seconds, I almost thought we'd be able to get away uninjured. When that one came for me, I thought that was the end.

That last guster would be the one to take him down. The way it shook him after it got a good grip... I shudder, trying to block out the memory. Damn it. God, I'm so ridiculously stupid!

Why did I leave the cave and wander out here like an idiot? I didn't just put myself in danger—I put him in danger too!

Now look at him. He's torn up and bloody because he had to save me from the mess I found myself in. He almost *died* because I was uncomfortable and bored while waiting in the cave. The worst of it is, it isn't like this is my first rodeo. I've lived here on Tajss for years. I know the dangers. I know how many things can kill me if I let my guard down for a second.

I know better. This was a rookie mistake at best. Guilt and shame swirl around, a toxic chaser to the fear of the encounter with the guster. I shudder, getting a flash of the guster's open mouth. Of the razor-sharp teeth inside that could slide right through flesh. That did slide right through flesh. Because of me.

Why the hell did he kidnap me? I'm a clear liability. Not only can I not survive on my own, I'm too stupid not to run headfirst into trouble. Worthless. Just worthless. I bet he's regretting the move now.

But the way he faced off against the biggest of them. Staring it down, growling, it was so… macho. Manly.

I snap back to reality when he stops moving. We're in the cave again, the shade a welcome respite from the unrelenting suns outside. It looks like he doesn't know what to do now. He is standing there, weaving. Like his only goal was getting us back to the relative safety of his home and having met it he's lost on the next action to take.

I shake my head. There's no time to wallow in self-pity or daydreams of how alpha he was. I need to get him cleaned up and assess the damage.

"Come on," I murmur gently, taking hold of his undamaged arm. Well, relatively undamaged. He has more than a few bruises speckled across his body, along with scrapes from the hot sand. "Sit down…"

I lead him over to the pallet, the only place to sit. He follows along, watching me with unreadable eyes as I get him settled onto the furs.

"Okay, let me just get some water, and we'll have you cleaned up in just a second."

DRAGON'S REDEMPTION

I go to the waterskins and grab a full one. There isn't anything to wipe him down with. He watches me curiously as I walk back over, taking a gentle hold on his arm.

"Let me just wash out the wounds," I murmur. I know he can't understand, but I hope the tone keeps him calm.

Angling it so the water won't drip onto the furs, I pour a steady, controlled stream across the puncture marks and tears. The blood is starting to clot, so I'm able to wash away most of it with the water and the palm of my free hand. I wince as the wounds come into full view.

That guster really tore into him, the teeth marks not at all crisp and even. They're more like jagged tears. A butcher job. A couple are deep enough that a needle and thread would be useful, but I don't have access to them. Hell, I don't even have access to clean bandages.

Pulling my shirt out of my trousers, I rip off a couple strips from the bottom. Frowning, I use the jagged bottom of my shirt to pat his arm dry before using the makeshift bandages to bind the wounds. I'm hoping they hold the edges of the worst wounds together tightly enough to help them heal cleanly.

I carefully wind the strips of cloth around his muscled forearm, feeling more in my element with something to do, with a way to take care of him. Feeling more in control of the situation, I notice things I shouldn't be noticing.

Like the smoothness, the softness of his intact skin, the way his scales lay onto each other. How hard his muscles are underneath my hands. The scent of clean male sweat that's coming off of him. Why is that so damn attractive?

I swallow, my hands slowing as I continue to wind the bandage, hyper-aware now of just how close I am to him. And how completely and utterly *male* he is. I glance at his defined abs, his hard chest, feeling that tug of attraction and heat low in my belly. I quickly look away, trying to ignore how my body brushes up against his as I lean down to tie off the bandage.

What is wrong with me?

Am I so damn lonely, so needy that I'll jump on anyone in the vicinity? Even a wounded male? And why would he want me anyway? I've clearly shown that I don't have two brain cells to rub together. Sure, I can bandage his wounds for him. But I'm the reason he got them in the first place.

Thoroughly disgusted with myself, I let my hands drop, glancing towards his face for the first time since I started working on his arm. His eyes are already locked on me, the look piercing and intense. The full force of his personality is behind those gorgeous, bright eyes. And it packs a punch.

I straighten and start to take a small, hesitant step back, my heart skipping a beat. But he doesn't let me.

I gasp as he reaches up, cups my face and pulls me back down. Right onto his lips. Oh. Oh wow.

10

JORMUND

*H*er slender fingers touch me with care, her touch delicate. Soft. Sensual. It takes everything in me to sit still and allow her to minister to my wounds. The pain of them is not important in comparison to the pleasure of her touch. The closeness of her body.

I breathe in her scent, taking her into my lungs as she works. I enjoy the closeness that I have not experienced since she woke, but this is so different from that.

When I held her, she was not awake and aware. Now, I can focus on the expressions that cross her beautiful face, see the way she frowns at the wounds, bites her plump lip while she cleans them. She is being so careful, trying to not cause me pain.

This close, I can admire the fine grain of her perfect skin, see the pulse in her neck fluttering. When she rips off cloth from her own garment, I catch a glimpse of the rich skin across her soft stomach, the delicate indentation of her navel.

My cock stiffens at the sight. At her closeness. The heat from her body. I want to strip her of the rest of her clothing, feast my eyes on that body. And touch her... everywhere.

I try not to make a sound as my cock throbs in response to my thoughts, my eyes dropping to skim over the soft curves of her breasts, her hips. The curve of her backside.

It is torture to remain still, not to act when she is so close. When she is touching me with those soft, careful hands. These desires are too intense, almost violent. I am not sure it is safe to be feeling them, but I do not know how to stop them.

I watch her pretty fingers tie the last knot around my arm. She looks up at my face for the first time since she sat me down on the furs. Her eyes are dark with a heat of their own.

I should not touch her, should not do too much when she is finally coming close of her own accord, but I cannot resist.

When she makes as if to step away, I reach up and cup the soft skin of her face, pulling her down to my lips. She makes a small sound, but she does not pull away.

I groan, slowly rising to my feet, opening my mouth so I can have more of her delicious taste. I am hungry for all of her. Starved for her touch.

The kiss is rough, rougher than it should be for our first kiss. My control is not what it should be. But she melts against me, her softness melting into the front of me, her breasts flattening against my chest, her heartbeat pounding against mine.

She kisses me back.

A burst of joy explodes within me at the soft motion of her lips, the delicate foray of her small tongue.

Yes.

More.

Warmth fills my chest at the sign of acceptance, an ignition of hope as I lower my arms and wrap my hands around her hips, knead her with my fingers. Perhaps... perhaps I could be worthy of this beautiful female.

Perhaps she could want me as I want her. Perhaps—

She stiffens against me and I stop. That lovely malleable softness turns to rigidity. Her mouth freezes against my own. Something is wrong.

She pulls away, ripping herself out of my hands though I do not try to force her to stay in my embrace. Her lips are swollen, her cheeks flushed, her eyes hot. The evidence of her desire is seemingly clear. But when she opens her mouth, her tone is not receptive.

I shake my head as she shouts, words I don't understand. I'm confused at this abrupt turn. She jabs her finger at me, her expression turning harsh. Gone is the soft, sensual female that I just held. In her place is a female who clearly wants nothing to do with me.

The warmth in my chest turns cold, extinguished under her rejection. I do not understand the words she uses, her language completely foreign to me, though it seems interspersed with words I think I should recall but I don't. All her words are sharp as my lochaber, cutting me deeper than the guster's teeth ever could have.

I take a step back, blackness swelling through my thoughts. An empty ache of despair swelling in my guts. She clearly feels wronged. I should not have touched her so roughly. Should not have mistaken her kindness for something more.

Guilt and remorse replace the raging desire, and I stare at her with no idea how to fix this. How to take back what I did. What do I do?

She continues her tirade against me, so I wait and accept it. But she cannot continue on forever. Perhaps she expected a response from me, but I do not yet have one. Her raised voice starts to lower, her agitated pacing slows.

Finally, she stops in front of me once more, simply meeting my eyes. Under the anger, I can see... hurt? Pain?

I stare back, wishing I could convey my remorse with my eyes. I never meant to hurt her. I would never hurt her intentionally. I open my mouth to say something, anything. But nothing comes, no words appear from the swirling darkness that my mind has become.

I have not used words in so long I do not even know how to reach for them anymore. Even if I could force them out, they might not matter. Might not make any sense to my treasure.

My shoulders slump under that realization, my helplessness a painful sting. I turn away, ashamed and saddened by how I managed to ruin the moment between us. She does not want me around her, that much is clear. No words are needed to convey that reality.

My wounds throb with pain as I walk out of the cave, not looking at her.

I must make this right, must fix this somehow. I pushed too hard and drove her away. It was clumsily done, but I refuse to leave the matter like this. Refuse to accept that she will forever turn from me now.

I must make it better. I will find a way.

11

DELILAH

$\mathcal{I}$ watch as he turns and walks away. Not just away from me, but completely out of the cave. Leaving me alone. Again.

Maybe I did too good of a job pushing him away. The cave is empty, too empty. I shouldn't have pushed him away, but damn it, I like it. I liked it too much. It was too intense and stupid. What the hell am I doing?

At a loss with the cave empty, I walk over to the furs and plop down on them, completely drained by my own outburst. I lie down and stare up at the ceiling.

Waiting.

Waiting for?

Waiting for him to come back, I guess. What else do I have to wait for?

He wouldn't leave me alone for long. Not again. Right?

And he's injured so he shouldn't be out hunting again. Right? It's only a few minutes before I'm fidgeting. My thoughts are racing. I can't lie still, can't find the refuge of sleep. I can't escape my own stupidity.

61

MIRANDA MARTIN

I make it a bit longer before, I sit up and go to the cave entrance looking outside for any sign of him. There's no sign of him. Now I have scarier thoughts.

Did he decide I was too much trouble after all? First, I put him in danger by wandering out of the cave straight into a guster pack. Then, when he tried to make a move, I shoved him away and screamed at him. What if he decided to leave forever? Just not come back to this burden he didn't realize he wasn't ready for?

Maybe he regrets taking me at all and decided to rectify the situation. I fall back onto the furs. The fact that I'm waiting for him to come back—that I want him to come back—is a clear enough indicator that I don't feel at all unsafe with him around.

I cover my face with my palms, taking in a deep breath. All right. I need to be honest with myself. It wasn't that I didn't like the kiss. Actually, it was of nice. More than nice. Maybe that right there is the real problem.

I wasn't prepared for the escalation. Or for my own reaction to it. Sure, I was discretely ogling him while I was bandaging him up—not my most shining moment, I'll admit. But admiring him and actual, sensual physical contact are two very different things.

I was shocked. Not only by having him pull me into a kiss. But by my reaction to that kiss.

My body went from the warmth of interest to an inferno of desire really freaking fast. Embarrassingly fast, I might say. I panicked. I panicked and took it out on the Zmaj.

The very same Zmaj who backed up as soon as I pushed at him, broke the kiss and didn't try to get close again while I yelled at him. He watched my tirade, his eyes wide. He didn't even run while I was yelling! He took the abuse quietly, letting me run out of steam on my own.

DRAGON'S REDEMPTION

And now I'm alone. And hornier than I ever remember being. Ugh. I turn over onto my stomach, beyond frustrated, both physically and mentally. All right, I have to believe he's coming back. So what do I do now?

What I really need is to distract myself. Rolling around on the pallet in a weird mixture of horniness and anxiety isn't helping. Surprise.

I get up off the fur, trying to ignore how hot and tingly I still feel. It isn't easy. Even just a kiss from the Zmaj was enough to light up every nerve ending. Once again, I start cleaning and straightening up.

I go outside, scoop up some clean sand, and dump it on the floor to soak up the spilled water I used to clean the Zmaj's wounds. Then I sweep it out. I straighten the furs. Then, I wander about because there isn't that much to clean in the cave. My wandering does result in a new find. The sun glints off something metallic in one of the cracks, drawing my attention. What is it?

I reach up and carefully feel inside, not knowing what I'll find. Sticking my hand into an unknown hole might not be the best idea, but here we are. Boredom really is the worst.

Feeling around slowly, I hit a smoothness that doesn't feel like the grit of rock. I wrap my hand around it and pull it out. I'm not surprised when I see it's a knife. A sharp little skinning knife, by the looks of it. I guess it makes sense to store it in a crack in the wall when there literally aren't any shelves or tables. Or even a basket or the like.

Hmm.

I turn the knife in my hand, admiring the sharp edge in the light streaming in from outside. Then I remember something else. There's a guster lying dead out there. I bite my lip, looking towards the mouth of the cave.

One thing I've definitely learned here on Tajss—you

shouldn't ever let anything go to waste if you can help it. The next meal isn't guaranteed. And guster meat is good. Not to mention there's a heck of a lot of it out there, waiting to be harvested.

The Zmaj already did the hard work. And shouldn't it have some kind of reward at least? I walk to the edge of the cave and scan the area outside. Of course it occurs to me that this is exactly how I got into trouble before. But what are the chances that the guster will come back after the last debacle? And their presence most likely scared other predators away...

I lean down to take a couple of the leather bags stacked near the exit, probably for this reason. I take a fortifying breath and step out.

The Zmaj isn't in great shape. I can at least help out by harvesting the meat. And he needs food to help him recover. My plan—if you can call it that—is to get in and get out as quickly as possible.

As I walk, I keep an eye out for any company. Either Zmaj or animal. But I don't see anything on the way, only sand and sun. I hesitate when I near the large carcass though. Staring at it, a chill runs through me at the sight of the body.

I could very easily have been the one killed rather than the beast. If the Zmaj hadn't heard me scream, if he'd been farther away...

I push myself past that hesitation. Fear like that is a luxury. I'm a survivor. The only way to get over it quickly is to dive right in. Here we go...

I wince when I make that first cut into the thick skin, half expecting the thing to roar back to life and snap me in half. But nothing happens. It's clearly as dead as dead gets.

I get into the zone, slicing through the skin and to the meat with an efficiency born of practice. If I'd known on the ship that I'd one day become an expert at field dressing an animal, well... I wouldn't believe it, but here I am.

DRAGON'S REDEMPTION

My mind wanders as my hands do the work of their own accord. It's comforting and familiar motions. And where does it decide to wander to? To the Zmaj of course. The most inconvenient place for it to go.

He really is quite a beautiful specimen of a male. Big and muscled, with those gorgeous lilac and blue eyes set in that strong face. Those big hands... and those soft, mobile lips...

I swallow as I think about his taste, the way he touched me, the small sounds of pure enjoyment he made. All of it telegraphing how much he wanted me. I like that. Liked that he wasn't afraid of making his feelings known. He wasn't trying to act unaffected.

Shit.

I shift, feeling the heat rising in me once more, but it isn't just the physical. It isn't just his looks that are attractive. All the Zmaj are pretty. And it's not just that he's been kind to me, kidnapping notwithstanding. All the Zmaj I've encountered so far have mostly been nice.

No, it's something else. There's something that makes him unique, different from the others I've come to know. Maybe it's because he's clearly hurting? Not physically, but inside. A past emotional wound. There's something sexy about a gruff, wounded man.

Or I'm just going crazy. Who the hell knows at this point? I clearly don't. All I know is that there's something about him that's got me all wound up. And I haven't felt that way about... anyone. Not this intensely. Not on the ship and certainly not here on Tajss.

I pack the meat away into the bags while I consider that. Not even the human men on the ship affected me this way. It's an interesting realization. One I'm going to have to think more on.

I shoulder the bags, grunting under the weight as I stand. I didn't harvest all the meat. It would be too heavy for me to carry back by myself. I cut off as much as I think I can carry. Even with that estimation, I'm cursing by the time I slog through the sand and up the path to the cave.

That isn't an easy journey without the added weight. A couple of times, I consider dumping one of the bags and coming back for it, but the thought of having to make this trip again stops me.

And I manage to make it, supply of meat in tow. Good job, me.

Setting it down on the ground to deal with in a bit, I wash up with one of the full skins of water the Zmaj left behind. I'm careful not to waste any, using just what I need to clean up and no more. There isn't a good supply of water here like there is in the Tribe's cave system.

I feel a lot better once I have the blood and bits of gore off. By that point, the suns are setting, the light slowly fading outside. I walk out to the mouth of the cave, looking down the path. Still no sign of the Zmaj. Sighing, I head back in. I don't know when he's coming back. I drop down onto the pallet, too tired to deal with the meat right then. I lie down.

And, with nothing else to do, my mind immediately takes a turn back to that kiss. There's a flash of heat, a heaviness between my legs. I fight it for a bit, trying to think of anything and everything else. But I've been pushing it away too long.

"Fuck it," I mutter, sliding my hand down the front of my pants.

I need to take care of this.

My fingers slide through my wet folds easily. I shudder at the touch, so turned on by that point that it feels almost like too much. I think about the Zmaj as I explore myself carefully.

About the breadth of his shoulders.

His gorgeous face.

His taste.

How big and thick his cock felt pressed up against me...

I arch up at that thought, my lust jumping to the next level. Oh God.

I close my eyes tight as I move my fingers faster. Harder.

12

JORMUND

I leap over the next dune, sliding down when I land on the other side. Snapping out my wings, I run as quickly as I can. I need to reach the oasis in record time. I will not have long to do what I want to do, so I must reach it fast.

I must fix the mistake I made, must make reparations for the boldness of my advance. I tried too much too quickly. I growl under my breath, digging deep and increasing my speed a bit more.

The desire that overcame me at her closeness, at her delicate touch... it was a sensation I do not remember ever feeling. That is no excuse for pushing where I should not have. All I want is for my treasure to be happy. To be comfortable and cared for.

All these years, I have been fighting to survive alone with no real reason to live. I have been doing what must be done and not thinking further than my next meal, for fear the abyss of nothingness would come up and swallow me whole.

Perhaps, though, there was a reason I survived. I picture my treasure's beautiful face. Yes. While I did not know why I fought so hard to survive. This is what I must have been waiting for, in the recesses of my brain that I cannot reach. Her. I was waiting for her.

She is the reason I did not die long ago. She is the reason I still exist. And the years I've lived this meager existence was the price to be paid to cherish someone as perfect as she. Beautiful, intelligent, industrious.

I have not been around her long, but her desire to be productive, the quickness of her mind, are very clear. As clear as her physical beauty. I will not ruin this gift I have been given.

The oasis appears in the near distance, the green a stark contrast to the red expanse of the desert sands. Good. I scan the area as I near. The water draws all kinds of creatures. I do not want to be taken by surprise. Especially not in my current bedraggled state.

I slow as I reach the edge of the lush greenery and trees and come to a stop. Scanning the edge of the oasis for any motion. It behooves one to tread lightly. There are many places for creatures—and dangerous plants—to lie in wait.

Something snaps to my right and I freeze, searching the shadows for the source. Nothing for a long moment then something scurries through the brush, but I see nothing. When no more sound comes from that direction, I continue on my path.

A branch lies along the path. As I step over, my foot crunches upon the dead leaves scattered along the other side of it. That crunch... my instincts scream to pull back, and I don't hesitate to react. I pull my foot back almost immediately after it touches down. There's the sound of movement, then a stalk of those desiccated leaves snaps around the place my foot just was.

I huff, eyes following the stalk over to the left. Pink and blue flowers grow along other stalks. The leaves are not actually dead—they are a disguise to lull creatures into thinking it safe. Once close, the selagi wraps around its prey, pumping out poison. Not deadly, but not at all comfortable.

I take a running leap across the branch instead, landing well past the dangerous area. The flowers have a seed in the middle that is edible if properly harvested but could make the recipient sick if not. I do not want to bring this type of flowers to my treasure. So I keep looking.

A bright orange catches my eye, but when I push some larger leaves apart, I realize it is a baby cvet. The interior of the massive plant is a stunning orange and red, very attractive. Designed to be so because the plant is carnivorous.

Even as I watch, its long, green tendrils snap closed around some small, furry animal that should have been more careful. It struggles in the plant's hold, the appendages wrapped so tightly around the small creature that I can only make out a shape as it nears the center of the plant. It's pulled inside and the struggles cease. The cvet has a paralytic poison that is very effective.

I step back, allowing the leaves to fall closed once more. My hunt must continue. It takes me more time than I would like to comb through the oasis until I finally find flowers that are the perfect gift.

Layas grow among the thinner branches of trees under very specific conditions. They require humidity and are only found in an oasis. They also require direct sunlight, so the branches of the tree they grow upon must be open to the sky above. In addition, a particular type of fungus must also share space upon the same tree. But though they are rare for these reasons, once harvested, they grow back faster than any other plant I have seen.

I scan the tree with two branches fully laden with oranges, pinks, and purples. Perhaps a combination of the three would be nice. The bark is rough under my hands as I climb up the tree. It sways slightly under my weight, but not so much that it concerns me.

I do, however, stay wrapped around the thick trunk rather than venturing out onto the thinner branches. Stretching, I reach out carefully with my knife to cut the first long, purple stem.

It detaches easily. I bring it close, admiring the overlapping petals that combine to make a fluffy, oval shaped flower with frilled edges. The stems match the color of the petals, heightening the appeal of the flowers. Beautiful.

Now that I have found them, it does not take me long to harvest a full bouquet of them. I make sure to shake them free of any small creatures before I bring them to my face. I breathe in deeply, closing my eyes. They smell as intoxicating as they look. I smile, climbing back down out of the tree and tucking them securely into my pack. An offering fit for my treasure.

The fruit of my hunt secured, I leave the oasis more quickly than I entered. I need to return to the cave. I do not like leaving her alone and vulnerable for a long period, so I travel as quickly back towards home as I did coming out. I am about half of the way there when some tracks give me pause.

Tracks that do not belong to any beast or creature. I examine them, my jaw tightening. Other Zmaj. A group of them. Her tribe is searching for her. I know this instinctively.

This is no coincidence. The tracks are too close to the cave. And they are not following the tracks of any possible prey. Nor are they going in the direction of a nearby water source. I ensure the tracks are not going in the direction of my cave before I continue on.

We will have to move elsewhere. I cannot risk them taking her. She belongs with me. My elation at finding the pretty flowers fades and worry sets in. The thought of

MIRANDA MARTIN

them taking her from me when I have just found her... no. No.

To make matters worse, the suns are setting. I push myself harder, wanting to be back at the cave before it is full dark. I manage to make it to the trail leading up the cave with light still in the sky. But then I hear something that sends a wave of renewed fear through me.

Moaning.

Coming from the cave.

I practically take the rest of the trail in one bounding leap, my hearts beating hard in my ears. I should not have left her alone. It was too dangerous, how could I have...

I pause before I barrel around and into the mouth of the cave. Wait. I still my breathing, listening intently to be sure. I hear another soft, low moan. It does not sound pained. Or distressed. But... pleasurable?

Swallowing, I peek around the corner to be certain. The sight sears into my memory. My treasure, on the fur, on her back. Her head thrown back in pleasure, her own hand between her legs, fingers working.

Clearly not in any danger or any pain. Quite the opposite.

My cock is hard between one breath and the next. I pull back, wanting to give her the privacy she deserves. I will not overstep boundaries again. I refuse to.

I take a few steps away from the cave, wincing as my cock throbs in complaint. I sit down, leaning back against the smooth rock next to the mouth. I let my head fall back, trying not to listen, not to make it worse.

I want relief. Badly. But it feels... wrong to use her private time to bring about my own pleasure without her permission. I will not abuse even the thought of her again.

So I sit outside, keeping my hands away from my cock. And try to think of anything else, my eyes moving constantly as I keep watch. It is an excruciating wait.

DRAGON'S REDEMPTION

Fortunately, she does not need much more time. I take a deep breath as I hear her cries escalate, her moans turning into gasps. And then silence.

I wait a bit longer before I rise to my feet, grimacing as I adjust myself.

But, to be sure, I deliberately stomp my feet, making more than my usual amount of noise so she knows I am coming. Nerves rising, I step into the cave.

13

DELILAH

I sigh as the pleasure slowly seeps out of my body. I really needed that. Sighing I stare up at the darkening ceiling, thinking over... everything. It's easier with the pressing physical needs met, my mind feels clearer.

Now I have to look at my own life. At myself and maybe it's time I be honest. Honest about my feelings and my own desires. The ones I've suppressed for so long. It's time to face how much I've been trying to bury my desire for a partner of my own. How depressed I've been getting around the other couples. How I've had to constantly reset my negative outlook to a positive one.

The kids. I love them, every one of them, as if they were my own, but every time I'm working with one of them, I ache. Zoe, with her cute as a button little face, the way she looks so serious when she's working something out.

The twins, picking on each other, but if anyone else bothers the other one, it's on. I chuckle thinking about those two. They're perfect, though I don't think I'd want to try birthing twins myself. That was hell on Mei. The Human-

DRAGON'S REDEMPTION

Zmaj pairings are hard enough on our bodies—twins was almost too much.

Aeros, Lana and Astarot's boy is growing fast too. As is Pachua, Maeve and Padraig's baby. Okay, I'm jealous! I can own that. How could I not be? The children are not only adorable, they're the future. They represent... everything. Home. Happiness. Hope.

Hope.

The kids are hope. Hope for a future. Hope for something more. Hope that there will be a next generation after us. And one after that. A better future.

How could I not want that? It's one of the primal drives of anybody, I think at least. The drive to make sure there's going to be a future. To make the world a better place for your own kids. I want my future too, damn it.

That future requires a man. Except I don't want just any man. I want a man who will treasure me, will care for me, one that I can connect with on a deeper level than only physical.

Right, well let's be picky, Delilah. Shaking my head, I snort. Could this Zmaj be the answer to what I want?

Despite the whole kidnapping thing? He's been nothing but sweet to me. God knows he's sexy—my current state attests to that. Maybe he's like Ryuth? Lost in the bijass, but he could be recovered, with the right woman's touch? With my touch?

Warmth forms in my lower belly, a different kind of warmth, at the thought. It's kind of... romantic, isn't it? A burly, sexy man, scarred by his past, all of which could be fixed by his love of the right woman?

That's the basis of a lot of the romantic vids I watched on the ship. Could it be?

End of the day, it's not like I have a lot of options either.

MIRANDA MARTIN

Not romantic, but it's the truth, and this is about being honest. Bluntly honest with myself.

If I want a future with a man in it, my options are limited. Well, I guess I could go to the City and find a regular, human guy. It might work. I mean, there could be someone there who would sweep me off my feet, make my heart race when I see him... there could be, but then there's this guy.

And he does make my heart race. He is sexy, sure, but more than that he's kind. Yes, he kissed me unexpectedly, but he's really only treated me with care and respect, even backing off the kiss immediately when I wasn't comfortable.

I could do a lot worse...

Loud footsteps outside the door jerk my attention to the cave's opening. Footsteps. Shit!

I quickly yank my pants up and refasten them, hopping up to my feet just in time. The Zmaj walks in as soon as I'm vertical. That was way too close!

My cheeks warm and I can't meet his gaze. Does he know what I was just doing? Damn, this is embarrassing. Like being caught for the first time exploring myself. He's stopped right inside the entrance, standing back a respectful distance. I can barely look at him all while trying to act nonchalant.

There's a splash of color in front of him so I put my attention on that. I blink, unable to believe my eyes. A giant bouquet of brightly colored flowers—pinks, oranges, purples. The heavy, frilly oval heads are downright gorgeous. Even the stems match!

I've never seen these flowers before. They're so breathtaking I just stare at them, stunned. Flowers. He brought me flowers? After I pushed him away, I was the cold bitch, and he goes and finds flowers.

On the ship this would be a minor gesture. How big of a deal could it be to go to a shop and pick up some flowers. On Tajss? Flowers?

DRAGON'S REDEMPTION

Suddenly I'm standing on a precipice looking into a dark abyss. Do I leap forward? Trust myself to fate and let my heart be at risk? Do I run away?

Oh man. I look up to his hopeful face, feeling terrible for having pushed him away, trembling. I really made him feel guilty for that kiss. A kiss that I actually enjoyed.

I made him feel so bad that he spent hours, braved dangers that weren't necessary in order to find these flowers. For me.

Slowly I walk closer. Feeling tentative, unsure, but I've never felt so bad for getting such a pretty, thoughtful gift. My hand trembles as I reach for them. His eyes meet mine. My mouth dries, and my heart leaps into my throat.

He moves the flowers closer to me, holding them with obvious care. Carefully not intruding into my space. The fragrant bundle rests between us, waiting to be accepted. His eyes plead, beg for forgiveness but I'm the one who needs to be forgiven.

"I... am... sorry," he says, his voice hoarse yet rich and deep.

Oh my God. I stare, my mouth agape in shock. Did he just speak? Did he just say actual words?

His voice was hoarse and gritty from disuse, but those were definitely words! The shock of it delays my response for a couple of seconds, but then I snap out of it.

"Oh, I mean, it's fine! Thank you for the flowers, they're absolutely beautiful, but, I mean, it's totally fine, you know? Nothing to worry about."

I mentally face-palm at the uncontrollable babbling. Smooth. Real smooth. In my defense, I literally just finished masturbating to thoughts of him. Having him appear right now is more than a little awkward.

He nods at my verbal diarrhea, his face relaxing. If I was holding out hopes for a full-blown conversation though, I'm

77

MIRANDA MARTIN

apparently out of luck. He doesn't speak anymore after I take the flowers, but he watches as I raise them to my face and inhale their soft scent.

They smell amazing, not quite like anything I've smelled before. As unique as they are beautiful. As unique as Tajss. As unique as the man standing in front of me. Broken and oh-so-damn sexy. It's as if I can feel his wound, calling to me, and somehow, I know I'm the balm for it.

An empty ache pulses in my core. We stare at each other, unsure of the next move. Part of me wants him to kiss me and this time I won't push him away. Yet another piece of me is afraid. Afraid to commit, afraid to give more than I'm ready to give.

He did kidnap me. Is this some kind of Stockholm syndrome? Or is it real? How do I know? He doesn't move except for his eyes. Those drop from mine then his jaw tenses, his wings ripple and his tail twitches.

He turns away and gathers up the furs that serve as both pallet and blankets, stretching them out. He gathers the waterskins and other small things in the cave laying them out in the center of the furs. When he gets to the bags of harvested meat, he pauses, staring at them with wide eyes. He looks over at me for a moment before continuing on with his packing.

Packing.

That's what he's doing. But why?

"What's going on?" I try. No answer. "Uh...are we going somewhere?"

I sincerely doubt he would bring me flowers and then leave me. Unless it was a goodbye gift? I have no freaking idea at this point. And he refuses to answer my questions. Or he can't. Maybe those three little words were hard won?

I watch him pack everything efficiently—not that it would take much time anyway, considering how few things

DRAGON'S REDEMPTION

there are—and then load everything on to his back. That's when he finally turns back to me. Slowly, moving deliberately with his eyes glued to my face he wraps a gentle hand around my wrist.

Looking for resistance? When I give him none, he nods and pulls me out of the cave. Down the path. And out into the dark, open desert. Oh no. This really doesn't seem like a great idea...

14

JORMUND

She doesn't resist as I pull my treasure gently out into the desert. I wish it was not nighttime. It is much easier for danger to hide in the dark. If I thought we had time, I would never travel with her after the suns have already set. But I must take her farther away from her tribe now. It is too much of a risk to remain in place when their tracks were so close. I cannot allow them to take her away from me.

"I don't know why we're traveling at night. If you wanted to suddenly embark on a road trip, fine, but we could have just as easily left in the morning, you know? And it isn't like it hasn't already been a full day—your wounds are still fresh, for God's sake! And—"

I listen to her voice as I move us quickly across the desert, enjoying the soothing tone of it. I love her voice even if the words make little sense to me. Her voice is as perfect as the rest of her. I wish I could understand more of her words. The fog, the bijass, slowly recedes. I found the words I needed to say to her. At least I hope they were the right words. They felt right and her reaction was good.

DRAGON'S REDEMPTION

I remember words, now. Once I spoke often. Once there were others... but something in me shies away and the bijass surges forward, clouding that thought. Now is what matters. I tighten my grip on her slightly. I cannot lose her. I cannot go back to my bleak existence before she came into my life. She alone is the reason I am coming back to myself. The reason I am becoming more than an animal who hunts, eats, sleeps. An animal only focused on surviving.

She is the most important part of my life and I will not lose her. I will not allow them to take her. I must stop them if they find us and attempt to do so. I would have no other option. However... I do not want to hurt them. I look at my treasure. She is healthy, both mentally and physically. It is clear her tribe was good to her, took care of her.

And I am grateful for that. Grateful that they took care of my treasure before I could. Before I even knew of her existence. Because of them, she survived until I could take care of her. I owe them a debt. I harbor no ill will towards them. They are not my enemy, but they will not feel the same. After all, how would I react if some strange male kidnapped my female? What action would I take?

It would not be a peaceful one. And I would not be willing to hear any kind of explanation. If her tribe finds us, I will likely have to hurt them to keep them from taking her. I do not know how my treasure will react to that. Yes, it is better if they do not find us.

She struggles through the sand making progress slow. I could carry her, but I don't want to push my luck. I don't know how she would react, and I don't have the ability to explain. So instead I do what I can to help.

Every sense strains as we travel. I'm alert to the slightest of changes around us. Ahead I see a rock formation that I recognize. I adjust our path based on it. My treasure trods along behind, not balking at the travel, though she keeps a

81

steady string of words coming. When I glance back her head is down, face covered with a sheen that reflects the light of the moon causing her to have a soft glow.

My hearts stop, my breath catches, and I quit moving.

Her beauty is captivating. I'm enraptured by the gentle lines of her face, the sharp intelligence in her eyes as her eyes rise and meet mine. The delicate curve of her neck, sweeping down to her shoulders. Her skin is rich in color her hair a beautiful coif that I want to twine my fingers in. Her lips are full, rich, and I desperately want to taste them again.

I can't. I won't. She hasn't accepted me yet. If I keep her safe, provide for her, sooner or later she will accept me. I know there is something wrong with me, some *thing* that means I am not good enough for her.

I must make sure I do not make a mistake. I must be sure I do everything right. I have to make myself be a worthy recipient of her love.

Behind the fog of the past that buries all my memories, something throbs and aches. Some failure, something I know was my fault. I did it. It was me, but what it was has been mercifully hidden from view.

My survival must have some meaning. It must. If not for her, my existence is futile. I cannot return to being alone. Living for no purpose other than surviving. I cannot return to a pointless, purposeless life. It cannot be that I survived for years for nothing. I do not want that to be true.

The empty ache throbs in pain. That ache has been my companion for so long, I didn't recognize it as something that wasn't part of myself. The bijass struggles to contain it. The memories almost come clear. Staring at my treasure, speechless, mouth dry, hearts bursting into a stampeding parade, it's almost there—but then it's gone.

Perhaps it will reveal itself in time, as my words are slowly returning. Perhaps it will never reveal itself, and I will

DRAGON'S REDEMPTION

forever carry this burden. I can do it. With her, with my treasure by my side, I can bear anything.

"What?" she asks, her head tilting to one side, hands on her hips, brow furrowing.

My lips twitch. I recognized this word! I know what she means. I open my mouth to respond, to express to her the storm of emotions raging in my heart, but when I do there is nothing but a blank where the words should be. Nothing comes out. I have no way to express my thoughts.

I snap my mouth shut, take her wrist, and turn away. My scales feel warm and itch, the bijass surges forward, and I struggle to not give into my basest instinct. Instead I move as quickly as I can across the sand, pulling her along with me.

Danger. There's danger around us. Her tribe is hunting us, wanting their female back, but she is mine. That's all that matters. The past is gone. Let it be.

My treasure.

The memories, the wild mix of emotions, and an underlying rage consume my attention. I scan the area around us, but I'm not aware enough. I know better than to move that quickly in the dark. Know better than to not be suspicious of not only the area around, but the area above and below us. I know better than to ignore the sand as a threat.

I know better.

But my desire to move quickly is too strong and this storm in my heart and thoughts is overwhelming. As soon as I feel the sand sink more than it should under my feet, I try to stop and back up, keep my precious treasure back from the soft spot. But I'm too slow.

The sand collapses underneath us. She yelps in surprise as the ground below us gives way, and we're falling.

I jerk her against my body and hold tight. Twisting as we slide and fall, bodies tumbling. I try to stop our perilous descent down, digging my free hand into the sand for some kind of purchase, but I find none.

I struggle, growling, trying to stop us. The sand is soft, sliding, and I find no purchase. We're picking up speed, falling faster and at last I abandon hope. Wrapping both arms around my treasure I curl my body around her much smaller, more delicate one.

She is more prone to injury than I. I cannot stop our fall, but I will protect her. The sand on either side abruptly gives way and we're in freefall.

It is dark, but I sense a greater space. Grunting, I twist our bodies, opening my wings and trying to turn the fall into a glide. There isn't enough room for me to open them fully. I can't slow our descent. Still we fall. I've no choice. Snapping my wings open, then shut, I'm able to turn us so that she's on top of my body. I close my wings around her protectively.

We fall for another beat. Then two.

My back hits the ground hard. I grunt as pain shocks me and the air is knocked out of my lungs. Loose sand still spills on us. Pushing past the blinding pain, I roll over, covering her with my body. I groan at the renewed pain in my arm. Everything hurts. I will not know my true injuries until I try to move.

I breathe lightly, quickly, almost panting, waiting for some of the pain to dissipate. I do not need to look around to know where we are. The zemlja, monstrous wormlike beasts, tunnel deep in the ground, creating vast networks that can destabilize the sand above. And I was stupid enough to lead us right down into one of those tunnels.

15

DELILAH

I'm following my erstwhile captor when everything happens. It's too fast for me to even scream. One second, we're rushing across the desert, the Zmaj taking most of my weight on his forearm, and the next, the ground decides to stop being the ground.

It happens so fast I barely gasp in a breath, preparing to scream. The Zmaj reacts much more quickly. He jerks me against his body and curls around me. My stomach is left somewhere far above as we drop.

He moves and scrabbles, trying to stop our fall, all I can do is wrap my arms around him and hold on, along for the ride. He twists, holding me tight as he does, his wings come out, or try to but there's not enough room. I'm watching him as time slowly crawls past. The fall becomes a parody of time moving. He looks down, his eyes meeting mine, and what I see in them makes my heart pulse harder and my breath catch.

Resolve. Love. Protection. That's the word. The fire burning in his eyes clearly communicates no matter the lack of words we have for each other. He will protect me, no matter what it costs him. Swallowing, lips trembling, I nod.

A rush of sensations like I've never felt before sweeps through me. An urge to kiss him bubbles out of the confusion of emotions and rising above with a burning need.

Stupid. We're falling, possibly to our doom, and I want to kiss him. My kidnapper. The sexy, strong, protective Zmaj who's done nothing but try to care for me. Kidnapping aside.

There's no time to act on the crazy impulse. The illusion of time moving slow disappears as it catches up in a rush. We slam into the ground with a crash. Hard. The air is knocked out of my lungs as we bounce with the impact only to slam down again.

His strong arms hold me tight, his body curled around mine, wings closed protectively around us. A generalized pain radiates throughout my body at the harsh impact. My thoughts are fuzzy, as if my brain has been knocked loose from its moorings in my head.

"Uffhh."

I struggle to get air back into my lungs. It won't come for the longest moment and my vision turns gray as everything swims. Finally the lock is lifted, and I pull in one lungful after another of the sweet air.

I carefully roll off of the Zmaj, not wanting to hinder his breathing either. If the fall hurt me that badly...

Closing my eyes I take a moment to assess any damage. I don't think anything is broken but it all hurts like hell. I try to rise but everything screams to stop so I collapse onto my back again. I don't hear him moving either. I need to check on him. He took the worst of the impact for sure.

I force myself to roll over to my knees and grit my teeth through the pain. The light is dim, almost non-existent, so I wait for my eyes to adjust, then crawl my way over.

His jaw is clenched, eyes tightly shut. There are wet-

DRAGON'S REDEMPTION

looking drops next to him. When I get closer I can tell that his arm is bleeding again. If that's the least of his injuries, I'll consider us lucky. Who knows what else is wrong with either of us?

"Why did we have to go out at night?" I ask. "I know you're well aware of all the dangers—what was so damned pressing! What were we running from?"

We had to have been running from something for him to move us with such urgency. In the dark, no less. At the sound of my voice, his eyes blink open.

Well, at least he's alive. That's good. I really don't want to be in this mess alone. I try to stand up to get some handle on where we are, but a sharp pain shoots through my right ankle.

"Ah, damn it," I curse, stumbling forward, and then falling again.

Shoot, shoot, shoot. Large hands grip me gently, easing me to a sitting position. He's close. So close, the scent of him fills my nostrils. The strength of his presence, his *there*ness is so masculine, so protective.

His strong grip on my shoulders, his eyes inches from mine, boring into me. His lips so close I could steal that kiss I wanted a few moments ago. He breaks his gaze and reaches for my ankle, but I shake my head.

"No buddy—at worst, it's sprained, I think," I say. I rotate the ankle carefully. It seems to be intact. I shake my head then put my hands on his chest. His muscle-bound chest, the swell of his pecs magical under my hands, but I push those thoughts aside and press him down. "Lie back down. You're bleeding again."

Those drops are now a small puddle next to him. I don't particularly want to see it grow any more. He looks surprised, but lies back down, his eyes focused on me while I redress the wounds. I'd like to wash them off again, but I can't see much

MIRANDA MARTIN

down here. It's bad enough using the same stiff, bloody bandage again, but my shirt can't spare any more torn off it.

The starlight shines through the hole above—the one we fell through—but the edges and corners of this cave are in shadow. I look away from them, not wanting to freak myself out over thoughts of what could be waiting in the dark.

Watching us. Okay, too late. Freaked myself out. I gently pat his shoulder, not knowing where he might be hurting.

"All done." He nods, sitting up once more. "We need to get out of this hole."

He looks around as he climbs slowly to his feet. He's moving slow, a lot slower than normal. His motions are stiffer than he was before. I take a deep breath of my own before attempting to stand again.

I make it up, but the pain is excruciating, causing stars in my eyes, before I make it to standing. He reaches down to help me to my feet, lifting me easily.

"Thanks," I murmur, slowly putting weight on my ankle.

It holds. So that's good. That sharp, initial pain gives way to a duller ache. I should probably rest it. Ice it actually, but we haven't had ice since the damn ship crashed here on Tajss.

"They want ice water in hell," I murmur and laugh at my own joke.

Tajss would pass for hell in most stories I've read. Besides, we're in a freaking hole in the ground. There is no ice and no time to rest. Rest can wait. When I look up, he's watching me with concern.

"I'm okay," I reassure him, patting his arms. His hands are still holding on to my elbows for support. "Let's try to find a way out of here."

He nods, watching as he lets go. When I take a step without help, he finally looks away. I lean on him, appreciating the support, as he scans the area around us.

DRAGON'S REDEMPTION

Can he see better than I can? I've noticed that the Zmaj have more than one eyelid. Or maybe it's a lens or something? If they're staring out across the desert, there's an inner lid thing that closes. I asked Astarot about it, and he said it takes the glare of the suns out. So it's a filter, which makes sense. Everything about the Zmaj is developed to survive in this desert. Do they have one for low light? Or better low light vision overall?

It's all pointless speculation, really. I'm curious is all. His head stops turning, and he moves to face me without removing his support. Carefully he puts his hands on my shoulders and steps away. He watches my face intently but I'm not sure what he's looking for. Me to balk? Pain?

Slowly he loosens his grip on my shoulders and only when I don't fall does he let me go completely. As soon as he's sure I'm standing on my own he looks up at the hole we came through. It's a long way up, farther than even his height has a chance of reaching. The Zmaj wings aren't designed for flying so there's no chance to fly out either. He does a fast perimeter walk of the space. It's obvious that he's looking for another way out.

Unsteady on my feet I do my best to help. My head is spinning, but if I focus, I'm okay. He's looking on the opposite side, so I inspect the wall closer. There seems to be one section that might have been an opening once, but it's completely caved in. Not helpful.

"What about this section?" I call out, staring at a rougher part of the wall close to where we fell in. "Maybe there's enough foot- and hand-holds?"

He comes over and inspects the section I gesture to. Nodding, he jumps up and grabs a couple of protruding rocks. They hold, and for a second I feel a surge of excitement. He's hanging in the air, then reaching for the next

89

MIRANDA MARTIN

handhold when they pull right out, and he drops down with the rocks in hand.

He hisses at the rocks in his hands, turns and throws them at the far wall.

"Yeah," I sigh, staring up at the night sky. "I hear you."

The most frustrating part of it all is that the exit is *right there*. Damn it. I walk over to the caved-in section. My head hurts so badly it's hard to think.

Maybe we could pile up some rocks to give us some height? Grabbing a smaller one, I bring it over to the hole. The Zmaj watches me with a curious look.

"Maybe we can pile them up? Use them to help us get higher up and climb out?"

I add gestures to the words to help explain. He nods, going over to the rocks and grabbing the bigger ones. Between the two of us, we're able to build up a pile. Standing back and inspecting it, I think it's high enough to get us out.

"I'll go first," I say.

He looks at me as if maybe he at least gets the general idea. I climb up the pile of rocks, but they slip under foot before I make it more than a foot off the ground. I'm about to reach a height of two feet when the entire pile collapses and I'm left in mid-air, pinwheeling.

He moves fast. Faster than lightning. One moment he's over there, then the next he's with me, grabbing me out of the air before I have time to fall. I'm resting in his arms, cradled against his chest.

My pulse speeds up, my cheeks warm, and I have to be free. I need space, I can't breathe this close to him. I struggle in his arms, needing to be put down. He doesn't fight me, setting me down and backing away.

Embarrassed, I can't meet his eyes. Biting my lip and staring at my feet, I do the only thing I can. I turn my back on him and stare at the rocks.

DRAGON'S REDEMPTION

"I'm going to make this work," I mutter.

Kneeling next to the pile I move some of the smaller ones around, trying to get the structure of it stable. He doesn't come closer, respecting my space, which I'm both thankful for and angry about. Why doesn't he help? I know why, of course. I'm sending mixed signals. What other signals can I send when I'm not sure what I feel or think?

All I know is right now I have to help get us out of this mess. I heave another rock up to the top of the pile, step back with quivering limbs and study it, nodding to myself that it is better. Not perfect, far from it, but better.

I start up, but this time, my foot slips and I fall backwards, taking a header down to the hard ground once more. His strong arm plucks me from the air and sets me down safely. I swallow, my heart in my throat.

"Thank you," I say hoarsely.

He nods, his hands still on my hips as he looks up at the hole. He meets my eyes once more, shaking his head, his own expression resigned. I frown. Is he giving up? His hands tighten on my hips, his eyes looking deeply into my own. There's something else in them now. Some emotion so strong it sends a shiver down my spine.

"My treasure," he says clearly, that gravel still apparent in his tone.

Treasure?

Before I have time to process it, he picks me up, shifting his hands so he can lift me well above his head. Up high enough that I can grab onto one of the more secure divots in the side of the hole. It should be a clear shot to climb out from there.

My heart melts. He called me his treasure. It hits me what he's doing and I'm not going to have it. No way, no how. Damn it, I've been alone so long I can't do this. I don't care if he kidnapped me. He's decided to save me, to sacrifice himself.

"No," I whisper, not reaching for the way out. "No." He pushes me up higher, his hands insistent. "No!" I say louder, struggling in his hands. "I'm not climbing out of here without you!"

It's the struggle that finally forces him to put me down or risk dropping me. He sets me down in front of him, his heart in his eyes. I stare into them, completely entranced.

There's an empty ache in my chest and it feels like a strong hand is tightening its grip. Impossible to get enough air. I'm losing myself in his eyes. Sacrificing himself, for me. For the small chance I'd survive out there alone. Or my friends would find me.

Fuck it.

I'm tired of trying to reason all of this out. Tired of weighing the pros and cons of the situation. Of figuring out what makes the most sense. I'm going with how I feel. This one time I'm throwing caution to the wind.

Resting my hands on his chest, I rise up onto my toes, moving closer. His eyes widen as I reach for his face, but then I place my lips on his.

I kiss him lightly. His top lip. Then his bottom lip.

Our breath mingles as I deepen the kiss, my tongue entering his mouth. He groans, his hands reaching down to cup my butt, hoisting me up so our height difference isn't an issue. Then he takes the kiss over, making it deeper, wetter. I moan, giving as good as I get.

The feel of his muscled chest and stomach against my own, the taste of him, the iron-hard length of his cock pressing against my belly, it's intoxicating.

Perfect.

It's like I'm drugged, my hands squeezing his shoulders,

DRAGON'S REDEMPTION

sliding into his hair, my body rubbing against his without thought. I want—

A hissing sound penetrates the haze that surrounds my mind and body. Abruptly, all that heat dissipates, and my hot blood runs cold.

We're not alone down here after all.

16

DELILAH

The Zmaj is against me, and I feel his body stiffen. Swallowing hard, I slowly turn my head and look over my shoulder. It's like a horror movie. The anticipation is almost as bad as the reveal.

Almost.

I have no trouble finding what made the sound. Glowing red eyes stare at me. *Big* glowing red eyes that don't need to blink. I blink, almost in response to that unrelenting stare. My eyes adjust and I try to look past those giant orbs to the thing they belong to. The Zmaj whirls us around and lets me go. Again, placing himself between me and danger.

I can't stop staring at it. Those eyes are set in the sides of a roughly triangle-shaped head bigger than the Zmaj, punctuated with slits at the nose and a longer, thin slit for the mouth. A long, black tongue slithers out of that slit, a hissing sound coming from the reptilian creature. As it makes the sound, two long flaps of leathery skin unfurl on either side of the head, framing it. A display of aggression, I'm willing to bet.

Its long, sinuous body is covered in a sheen of reddish

scales, punctuated with darker brown swirls along its hide. It's thick, too thick for me to get my arms around it. At least a meter in diameter.

I follow the curved line of its body through the cave, trying to find the end. I don't find it. Some of it is still inside the hole it came through. The hole we started by grabbing rocks from the cave-in to try to get out of this place.

The noise we made must have alerted this thing that there was prey nearby. He crouches, grabbing his lochaber and moving closer to the... snake? It feels weird to call it that, but that's what it looks like. A giant-ass snake.

"Why'd it have to be snakes?" I mutter to myself, shaking my head, chuckling at the reference.

It's not that I'm not scared, I'm terrified. I don't know what else to do with the fear. Those cold, red eyes flick to me at my slight movement, the thing's head bobbing hypnotically in the air.

The Zmaj creeps closer, moving smooth and low, the lochaber held across both hands, like a staff. One second, the giant head is barely moving, shifting slowly. The next, it's darting at the Zmaj, so fast it's a blur of movement.

I gasp, my heart in my throat. The Zmaj leaps away just before the head reaches him, and his lochaber whistles through the air, slicing the snake's cheek. The snake hisses, and its mouth unhinges revealing long, sharp fangs.

I gulp, looking down the barrel of that mouth, into the dark depths of its gullet. It's big enough to swallow even the Zmaj whole.

Unfortunately, even I can see that the slice the Zmaj landed was only superficial. All it did was irritate the thing.

Unthinking I take a step forward as it strikes again, but stop myself, fear, anger, all overridden by a desire to help. I can't get closer. All I'll do is become a target myself and split the Zmaj's focus, making him more vulnerable to attack.

That's what happened with the guster herd, and I won't repeat the same mistake.

The thing strikes, fast, twisting its body around in a crazy, impossible way. The Zmaj barely manages to avoid the strike. He leaps up and over, feet touching the side of the cavern and pushing off. He flies towards the thing from the side, lochaber held ready to strike. He's aiming for the thing's head, a deadly strike if it connects.

The sharp blade cuts right across one of its glowing red slit-pupil eyes.

The creature hisses loudly. It echoes off the stone walls, a harsh sound that makes the hair on my arms stand on end. Its head jerks back from the pain as the Zmaj lands in a crouch in front of it.

Fluid runs down from its ruined eye, its mouth is open halfway as it recoils from the source of the pain. At least, that's how it looks, but it proves to be a ruse.

One second, it's flinching back, and the next, it's darting back in.

Unfortunately, the ruse works. The Zmaj isn't quick enough to avoid it.

"NO!" I cry out as its head darts in, certain this is it.

Surprisingly, the thing doesn't bite him, and for an instant my hope blooms. I don't know why it didn't bite until an instant later as its body moves in tandem with its head. It coils around the Zmaj's body.

Shit. It's trying to strangle him!

It's around him in the blink of an eye. I can barely see him past the thick coils. Only the back of his head is now visible. The monster's scales have a wet look, and I can see them flexing as it tightens its body around its prey.

"No," I whisper, taking another step closer.

He's always put himself in danger for me. Thrown himself into the deep end for me. This can't be how he dies. It can't be. Not when I'm starting to feel... things. Not when I just found him!

I look around for something, anything to help... the rocks!

There's a whole pile of them here thanks to that earlier attempt to escape. Crouching down, I grab a hefty one, quickly weighing it in my hands. The head is visible, though it's facing away from me.

Taking a deep breath, I wind up, hoping my aim is good. The Zmaj is struggling silently, the coils around him shaking but not budging. I only have to distract the thing...

I grunt, flinging the rock as hard as I can. Hoping it's enough to do *something*. The rock soars through the air, seeming to slow as it moves through the air towards the monster, but it's on track to hit.

The rock smacks into the back of the snake thing's head with a thud. It jerks, hisses loud enough that it echoes around me, and its head whips around lightning fast, cold eyes locking on to me.

Uh oh.

I step back, wondering if I have signed my own death warrant. It stares at me and I stare back, my heart in my throat. Right when I expect it to dart forward and end me, it turns away, its mouth opening up in another pained hiss.

I look for the reason and see the tip of the Zmaj's lochaber pierce through one of the coils holding him in. The snake must have loosened its coils giving him more room to maneuver!

Hope grows in my chest as he stabs through the coil again, the creature's hold on him loosening farther. When there's enough room, he leaps straight up out of the hold. The Zmaj rises into the air, wings spread, roaring. He's like a scaled angel, rising into the sky.

The creature's open mouth follows, just beneath him, reaching. He doesn't make any move away as he continues his arc into the sky, the monster chasing him. I want to scream, warn him, but I open my mouth and no sound will come out. Is he going to be able to avoid it?

He doesn't even try.

As the mouth comes closer, he lands on the open mouth with one foot on the thing's nose and the other on the lower jaw. He pulls his lochaber back and plunges it deep into the already-ruined eye.

There isn't another hiss of pain. It falls over, muscle control gone. It's over. I take a step closer.

"Delilah!"

I freeze at the sound of someone yelling my name. From above.

What in the hell...

17

DELILAH

*I*t's a long, frozen moment in time, as I look at my Zmaj captor. There's something in his eyes, written on his face, that I don't know how to identify. Is it disappointment? Anger? Regret? All of that and more?

He doesn't move. Doesn't look up, refuses to take his eyes off of me. Almost it's as if he's pleading with me, but silently. As if he's begging me not to call out, to say nothing, to stay here with him. Remain trapped in this hole and not return to the world I know.

An ache forms low in my stomach, and I almost want to. Almost.

"Delilah!" the voice calls out again, but this time I recognize Ragnar's voice.

My decision is made for me right there. No matter how torn I'm feeling, no matter how kind he's been to me, he *kidnapped* me. My friends, my family are worried about me and won't stop looking. I don't know what's going to come next, but first things first, I'm going to get out of this damn hole.

MIRANDA MARTIN

"Here!" I yell, looking up, squinting to try to see. "Down here!"

The shape of a head and shoulders appears over the edge.

"Ragnar!" I cry out, so relieved at the sight of his familiar face I almost start crying. "It's so good to see your face!"

Luckily, I manage to hold it in for the sake of my pride.

"We could say the same," Ryuth says, his head appearing next to Ragnar's. "We have been looking for you for days now."

Olivia's head pops over the edge of the hole next.

"It's so good to see you in one piece, Delilah!" she says, waving.

"Me too!" I laugh.

"Can you climb out?" Ragnar asks. He frowns deeply as he scans around the rest of the cavern. "Is that a dead kigyo? How did you manage to—"

He cuts off mid-sentence and his face hardens. He's seen the Zmaj, standing in the shadows behind the body of the kigyo. Tension fills the air and Ragnar hisses softly.

"Delilah—" he starts.

"He killed it," I say cutting him off before he can say more. My erstwhile kidnapping Zmaj isn't looking at the two members of the Tribe with a warm expression either. "He saved my life."

Ragnar and Ryuth share a look. I don't know what it means, but it doesn't look good. I can almost see them decide to put the matter aside, for now at least. They murmur between themselves for a minute or two before turning back to us.

"Can you two climb out?" Ragnar asks.

I look at the Zmaj down here with me. I wish I knew his name. It would make him more... human? More... friendly? I don't know, less of a thing, more of a someone, I guess. I hate

DRAGON'S REDEMPTION

thinking of him as only 'the Zmaj' or 'kidnapper'. He meets my gaze, silent and stoic, but he doesn't respond.

I motion up to the hole, miming climbing out when he doesn't respond to that. He shakes his head negative in a subtle motion. I frown but he doesn't say or do more. Resignation is what I would call it. He's resigned himself but he's not happy about it.

"No," I call out, not taking my eyes off of him.

"Step farther back, away from the hole," Ryuth says.

I do as I'm told, stepping well back. I look up at my Zmaj's face, but he's focused on the others now, his body tense.

"It's okay," I murmur. "It's going to be okay."

He gives me a brief glance, but doesn't acknowledge the words. I sigh and maybe stupidly move closer to him. His entire body stiffens in response. He doesn't know what to do with it, and I don't know what to with him.

I sigh. I don't blame him. This is an awkward situation at best. Slowly I touch his arm, his eyes focus on that point of simple contact. His muscles thrum with pent-up energy. He's vibrating under my touch.

I turn my attention back to the hole at the sound of small bits of rock and dust dropping down. What are they doing? I crane my neck to see better. Oh.

Ragnar is holding Ryuth's legs, dangling him as far into the hole as he can. Ryuth is stabbing his lochaber into the firmly packed earth and rock surrounding the hole. He continues until he drives it in, and it sticks deep without the earth crumbling around it.

"It is secure," Ryuth calls back to his brother, wiggling the lochaber's handle to demonstrate.

Ragnar nods, letting go of Ryuth's legs. Ryuth holds on to the shaft of the lochaber, legs swinging as he drops down.

I hold my breath, wondering if it'll hold. It does. Ryuth

moves so his feet are braced in divots beneath the lochaber handle, removing one hand from it.

"Ready!" he calls up.

Ragnar carefully slides down the hole, using the side that isn't as steep. His legs swing in the open air until they come to rest on the lochaber handle. Ragnar takes his lochaber off his back and hands it to Ryuth.

Dangling from one hand Ryuth uses Ragnar's lochaber the same as he did his own. Driving it in until at last it finds solid purchase. Once he's satisfied it's solidly set, he gets his feet onto it. Somehow, he manages to hook his legs over the handle and dangle down, reaching with his arms. He's still pretty high above the bottom of the cavern, though he's near the bottom of the hole we fell through.

"Can you reach me now, Delilah?" he asks.

I step over to where he's hanging, gauging the distance. I really don't think so, but I try anyway. My fingertips aren't anywhere near his, even if I try jumping.

"No," I say, frustrated.

The word barely leaves my lips before I feel big hands wrapping around my hips and lifting me up. The Zmaj. Ryuth's face is grim as he grips my outstretched hands. As soon as he has a secure hold, he bends his arms and raises me up.

"Try to get on top of the lochaber," he orders.

I nod, scrambling up the rest of his body to the handle. It gives under my extra weight, making my stomach queasy. I try not to think about how much weight it's holding.

Pressing myself against the dirt wall I stay crouched, keeping my head up, not looking at the ground. Ragnar reaches down from the lochaber above me and grips my shoulders.

I hold my breath as he picks me up, lifting me easily. The lochaber he's on bends an alarming amount as he lifts me

DRAGON'S REDEMPTION

onto it with him and I have to close my eyes to keep from getting sick.

"Climb onto my back," he orders.

"I can't," I say, scared to even open my eyes.

I can't do that. I can't move. We're going to fall again any moment and this time I won't be so lucky on my landing. I won't have the strange, kidnapping Zmaj to protect me from the impact. I'll be screwed this time.

"I know it's scary," he says, his voice reassuring. "Delilah, you can do this."

Biting my lip, eyes closed tight, cold sweat sliding down my spine, I nod.

"Right," I exhale. "Right…"

Slowly, I blindly reach for him until I find him by touch alone. Terror threatens to freeze me in place, and I'm doing all I can to not give in to it. Slowly I feel my way around him. His scales are cool to the touch as my fingers slide over his massive arm muscles. Around, onto his back, and then I come up against his folded wings.

"Okay," I mutter, wrapping my arm over his shoulders.

This is it. Do it. We're high up now, but I have to be brave. Push through it. In a single, blind motion, I whip myself around him, tightening my arm into a death grip around his neck as I do.

"Delilah," he whispers in a strained voice.

"Sorry," I apologize, forcing myself to loosen my grip on his neck.

"Move between my wings, please," he says.

I shift myself, still too scared to open my eyes. The shaft is bending beneath us and I swear I hear the wood slowly cracking.

"This?" I ask, eyes clenched tight.

"Fine," he says. "Hold on."

He doesn't give me any more warning. Flaring his wings,

MIRANDA MARTIN

he leaps up, and my stomach is left behind us. I scream, unable to contain it. There are sounds, barely heard over my scream, of dirt falling and exclamations from Olivia then all the motion stops.

I'm on solid ground. Or as solid as a planet full of sand can be. We're out. Ragnar pulls me off his back and sets me down on my own two feet. I open my eyes, looking around, but my knees are weak and shaky. I flop onto my back, taking a deep breath. I've never been so happy to feel sand against my back.

"Here," Olivia says, offering me some water. "That did not look like an easy climb."

I shake my head, taking a few sips.

"I wouldn't want to do it again," I agree.

"We are up!" Ragnar calls out to Ryuth.

"I am coming!"

Wait. I scramble over to the edge of the hole.

"Careful, Delilah! You'll fall back in!"

Olivia grabs me by the waistband, but I'm too focused on the fact that Ragnar is trying to come up alone.

"Wait! You have to help him get out of there too!"

"He kidnapped you," Ryuth hisses. "Let him rot in that hole."

"He does not deserve our help," Ragnar agrees, glaring down at the silent Zmaj.

He doesn't try to defend himself, watching impassively.

"I gotta say, I agree with the guys on this," Olivia murmurs.

"No," I return, digging in my heels. "He's the reason I'm alive. You have to help him get out."

I glare at Ryuth and then at Ragnar. They exchange another look, clearly exasperated, but I don't care, so long as they relent.

"Delilah—" Ragnar says.

DRAGON'S REDEMPTION

"No!" I yell, rising up to face him. "No, just no. He comes too."

Ragnar backs up from my onslaught then nods.

"Of course," he says, after exchanging a look with Olivia.

Ryuth holds his hands out for the other Zmaj. He reaches them without issue, climbing onto the lochaber and leaping to the next one himself. And then right out of the hole. He's up and out in a fraction of the time it took me.

Ryuth must have a fire under his ass because he's up on the other Zmaj's heels, lochabers in tow. At least we're out of the that damn ho—

"No!" I cry out as the Zmaj attacks our rescuers. "Stop!"

He doesn't stop, though, his lochaber spinning expertly in his hands as he stabs at Ryuth. Ryuth barely dodges the blow, catching the lochaber Ragnar tosses at him.

Why is he attacking? I keep out of the way, afraid to be caught in the cross blows, watching in horror as they all go at each other. Fast. All of them are so fast.

Ragnar and Ryuth land blows, but so does the Zmaj, his wings flaring as he leaps, his muscles tensing and flowing as he dodges and attacks. Ragnar and Ryuth try to trap him between them, but he attacks Ragnar directly, swiping his feet out from under him, avoiding being cornered.

Ragnar is bleeding from a slice to the arm, my Zmaj is sporting the beginnings of an ugly bruise on a cheekbone, and Ryuth is favoring his side.

What the hell is the point of this! They start at each other again.

"No!" I scream, daring to get closer even as Olivia fights to keep me back out of harm's way. "Stop! Now!"

Something in my tone has my Zmaj turning his head towards me. He meets my eyes, the emotion in them so deep it hurts my heart. He drops his lochaber. I stare, taking in his defeated expression, but there isn't time to keep staring.

Ryuth slams the butt of his lochaber across the face. Ragnar follows up with a punch to the defenseless Zmaj's stomach.

"Stop it!" I scream.

I rush over, trying to grab at them as they beat the poor Zmaj down. It's two against one. The Zmaj starts to fight back, but he's also already wounded. It's far from a fair fight. And I stupidly had him drop his lochaber. Tears stream down my face as they beat him to the ground, ignoring me.

"He's down!" I scream, slapping at them. "He's down!"

The Zmaj shakes his head, trying to get back up. He falls back to the sand, blood streaming from a split lip, the beginnings of a black eye coloring his face. There are a few more cuts and bruises added to his already-wounded body.

Ryuth and Ragnar finally stop when they realize he can't get up. Olivia looks on with a simultaneously confused and horrified expression. It isn't fun to see anyone beaten down.

"Fine," Ragnar growls. "Let us return home."

He wraps an arm around my waist, pulling me away. Fast. I turn to look over my shoulder.

"Delilah," the downed Zmaj calls out, reaching a hand towards me.

I can almost hear my heart shatter in my chest. But...

Maybe these feelings aren't real. He did kidnap me. They aren't wrong about that. Maybe the situation affected me more than I realized. Maybe I don't really know how I feel...

I bite my lip. Damn it, I need time to think!

"Wait," I ask as they drag me along with them.

"No," both Ryuth and Ragnar say in unison.

"We will only have to hurt him more if he attacks again," Ryuth adds grimly.

Olivia looks over at me from her place in her mate's arms.

"Let it go," she says in a low voice. "Getting them close to that Zmaj isn't a good idea right now if you don't want him to take another beating."

She has a point. They're still pumped up on adrenaline and anger. I nod, looking back again, but we've gone over a dune.

I've already caught my last glimpse of my former kidnapper. I still hear the sound of my name on his lips.

He called my name. He spoke. The second set of words he's ever said to me and they broke my heart into a million pieces. Now I need to know, is there something there for us?

18

DELILAH

*R*yuth carries me easily in his arms and we track as quickly as possible. It's not as fast as it would be in the light. That's how I got dumped into that cavern in the first place. Still we're moving fast. It's obvious they want to get as far from the Zmaj who kidnapped me as possible.

I can't keep myself from looking back though. Is he okay? They beat him really badly, and he was already hurt to boot. Now he's alone in the desert, near helpless, bleeding, prey for anything that comes along.

Am I insane? Is this some weird Stockholm syndrome? Am I so lonely that when the first and only eligible male comes around, I'll forgive all the bad things he does for a shot at having someone of my own?

Sure, on the surface, it was bad. He took me against my will. Kidnapping is bad, of course, but if I look at it from his side, it makes sense. I know enough of the Zmaj to know what happens to them if they're alone too long.

They lose themselves to that mental state they call the bijass. It's foreign to me, but what I understand of it from studying them and living with them is it makes them primal.

DRAGON'S REDEMPTION

Regressive in a way, very alpha male, caveman-like, I guess. It's obvious that my kidnapper was deep in his bijass.

As deep as Ryuth once was, and he's carrying me now. He's fully integrated back into our new society, and not only a functioning member but the mate of Mei.

"We will stop here," Ragnar announces, pointing towards a low grouping of rocks that can act as a shelter.

"Good," Ryuth agrees. "We can continue on in the morning."

"Are we close to the Tribe yet?" I ask.

They both make negative sounds.

"We have some way to go yet," Ragnar tells me. "Your kidnapper managed to take you quite a distance."

My kidnapper. It's a fact. But then why does the title feel so wrong? God, there's no easy answer to this. We set camp up quickly, starting a fire and setting out pallets. They have provisions ready, so at least no hunting is necessary yet.

I chew on the well-seasoned jerky, staring at the fire. Trying to make sense of all the conflicting emotions inside me.

"How did he take you?" Ryuth asks out of nowhere.

"Huh?" I look up at him.

"How did he kidnap you?" he asks again. "We were nearby. We should have heard you scream or at least heard a struggle."

Ah.

"You were there one second and just gone the next. Poof!" Olivia adds, shaking her head. "You weren't going far—I thought it was safe. Or that I'd at least hear you if something happened."

"It isn't your fault. He was waiting in the water," I explain. "When I went to fill up my waterskin, he pulled me in."

"No way to scream underwater," Ragnar murmurs. "Clever."

MIRANDA MARTIN

"And any struggle would also be silent," Ryuth agrees. "He thought it out quite well. We will have to take better care in the future."

"What happened after he took you?" Ragnar prods.

"Well... I woke up in a cave."

"You woke up in a cave?" Ragnar repeats. "Do you know how long you were unconscious?"

I shift, uncomfortable at the line of questioning.

"No," I mutter. "I don't."

"If she was out, there's no way she could have been timing it," Olivia points out.

"After you woke, what happened?" Ryuth probes, leaning forward.

"He took me to his home. He made sure I had food and water. He hunted for us." I skip over the part with the guster —they don't need to know that. It was my fault anyway. "Then something scared him, and he wanted to leave during the night. That's how we found ourselves in that hole, with the giant snake thing."

"I am sorry we did not keep you safe," Ragnar remarks solemnly. "I am sorry you had to endure such an ordeal."

Ryuth murmurs his agreement.

"I'm never looking at water the same way again," Olivia adds.

I shake my head.

"It wasn't bad. He kept me safe, made sure I had food and water—"

"He kept you alive. For his own purposes," Ryuth inter-rupts, darkly.

"Yes, do not mistake whatever he did for you for kind-ness," Ragnar agrees. "When we couldn't find you in the oasis and then saw the tracks...we were frightened for you."

I want to keep disagreeing with the solemn tone they've taken, but they clearly don't want to hear it. I don't blame

DRAGON'S REDEMPTION

them. I'm touched that they care so deeply about me, that they kept searching for this long, came this far out to retrieve me. And I appreciate that they were scared for me. Heck, I was scared for me too!

But... they obviously think they know best. No matter what I feel my actual experience was like. I'm not sure whether I'm right or they are. He did kidnap me.

Like Ryuth did with Mei...

He cared for me, treasured me. He called me his treasure. The words echo through my thoughts, the sound of his voice, rough and scratchy from disuse.

"Thank you for looking for me," I say instead of arguing.

"Of course," they both say in unison. "You are Tribe," Ragnar adds, smiling. "I know everyone will be quite happy—and relieved—to see you."

"We couldn't go back without you," Olivia says, leaning over and hugging me. "We have to keep each other safe out here."

I hug her back, taking comfort from the embrace even while my emotions flip flop.

"Wait—we should have given this to you right away," Ryuth says, reaching into one of the bags.

He pulls out a small bundle of leaves. I know immediately what it is, and my body cries out for it. All the stress has kept enough adrenaline running through my body to hold the withdrawals at bay, but the moment I see it they're there. My muscles tremble so badly I can't reach for it.

Epis. It's best when eaten fresh—I don't know how long they've been carrying it around—but I definitely need whatever I can get. He holds it out, and I grab it, greedily shoving a piece in my mouth.

A sour, spicy flavor bursts in my mouth. I chew it, a sigh of relief leaving me as a chill sweeps through my body, the plant literally cooling me down. The body pain, the headache, the stomach cramps and slight nausea that's been intensifying goes away.

Swept away by the epis. I know it's changing me on a cellular level, changing my DNA so I'm better adapted to the conditions here on Tajss. And forever tethering me to this planet, the only place to find the addictive plant. That gave me pause when I first took it.

The thing is that it keeps us humans all healthy here. And, realistically, we have no way off this planet without a spaceship. There isn't going to be a rescue from Earth or anywhere else. Even if they tried, it would take generations to get here.

If we built a ship, out of what I have no idea, there is nowhere to get to within in our lifetime. That's one thing I'm grateful for—those of us who survived got the chance to breathe fresh air here, not the recycled stuff we inhaled our whole lives on the ship.

Closing my eyes, I sigh and enjoy the sensations of health.

"Better?" Olivia asks in sympathy.

I nod emphatically.

"I don't know how much longer I could have gone without it. Thank you," I murmur.

"Of course," Ragnar responds. "I'm only sorry it took us so long to track you down."

I shake my head. "Don't be ridiculous."

"Be that as it may," Ryuth steps in. "We should all get some rest while we can. Ragnar—would you like first watch or second?"

"I will take the first one. You three rest. We will have a full day of travel tomorrow."

I nod, lying down in one of the pallets while Ryuth lies in the other. Olivia settles into the pallet next to Ragnar as he stations himself so he can look out at the desert around us.

My eyes are heavy, my thoughts dull, and I want to sleep.

DRAGON'S REDEMPTION

Exhaustion lies heavy on my body, but my mind won't stop running through everything that's happened in the last few days. The kidnapping, the guster, the cavern, and the snake thing, sure.

More though, the flowers. The kisses. It's as if I've lived a whole other lifetime in the last few days. One that's taken me through a whole roller coaster of emotion. I can't stop seeing that look on his face when he quit fighting Ragnar and Ryuth.

For me. He stopped for me.

I saw how hard that was for him. He didn't want to stop, that was obvious. Every instinct in him was to keep fighting, and he might have won, too. He was holding his own against them, for sure. He didn't want to, but he did. Because I wanted him to.

Some strange, metaphysical, emotional parts of me are shifting. Part of me that I don't understand, things I sense, more than I can point to or call out. A block, a barrier, something that was stopping me from going all the way with my feelings.

Suddenly I have a burst of clarity lying here on this pallet. It all comes clear, and at last, slow as I may be to see it, it all makes sense. The storm of emotions, the reactions, and I'm certain. At last I know, beyond shadow of a doubt, where I stand.

I love him.

Maybe he did everything wrong, but that doesn't mean he's a terrible person. It definitely doesn't mean his heart was in the wrong place.

Kidnapping aside, he was nothing but gentle, caring, even solicitous towards me. He cares. It's there in every action he's taken for me. And I left him behind. Left him behind to fend for himself while he's hurt.

My cheeks burn as acid rises in my throat. I should have

fought harder, should have insisted more. I can't believe I left him, alone, hurt and uncertain. He probably thinks I hate him.

None of that will help me now. I have to remedy the situation, fix it. But how?

Rolling onto my side I stare at Ragnar, fully alert and watchful. He would never let me wander out into the desert alone, especially not to go find the Zmaj they beat senseless. Neither of them would be okay with going back to find him together. They've made that quite clear. In their minds, he's written off for the kidnapping.

Not that that's fair in the slightest. Ryuth kidnapped Mei originally. Sverre kidnapped Jolie soon after we crashed, and now they're pillars of the community. Maybe I could make an argument that would get Ryuth's support?

Or not. They understand the bijass better than I do. And they're brothers who have a connection that is stronger than any other Zmaj I know. I don't think I'm going to be able to change their minds. My kidnapper has offended their honor. He took me on their watch.

Okay.

I have to slip away, alone. Now, before we move even farther away, and I have to back track even more. At some point, Ragnar and Ryuth have to switch watch. So I watch Ragnar and wait.

Now that I have a plan and a purpose, time drags. I listen to the soft breathing of Ryuth and Olivia. They stir and shift, rolling over. Ragnar's head makes a constant scan, left slowly moving right, until he's gone as far as he can before slowly scanning the other direction.

The stars shift overhead. Soft breezes switch directions. Insects chirp and the small fire crackles as the moments continue to drag past. I'm about to do something stupid. Really, really stupid. Too-stupid-to-live stupid.

DRAGON'S REDEMPTION

Or brave.

The bravest, most daring thing I can do. I'm going to find him. My kidnapper. Somehow, I don't think he'll be far away. I hope.

I'm smart enough to know how to survive out here for a while, but sometimes it's not about being smart. Sometimes it comes down to brute strength, and if I get into one of those situations, I'm up the proverbial creek.

I have to do this, though. I know it now. He was changing for me, he was coming back to himself, and I want to know that person. The one I saw glimmers of, in his words, sure, but more in his actions.

He never hesitated to put himself in harm's way to protect me. Me. He called me his treasure. My entire body warms as his voice echoes through my head again. Damn it why won't time hurry up and pass!

At long last Ragnar rises from his station and moves towards Ryuth.

"Ragnar," I whisper.

He turns to me, obviously startled to see I'm awake.

"Yes? Is something wrong?"

"I can't sleep," I explain. "Might as well let me take second watch so Ryuth can be rested tomorrow. I mean, you guys are doing all of the heavy lifting."

Literally. He hesitates, looking over at Ryuth.

"Don't worry—I'll wake you if I see anything even a little questionable. Okay?"

He frowns, his brow furrowing as his jaw tightens. He shakes his head.

"I do not think this is a good idea," he says. "Ryuth will be fine."

"Ragnar," I say, sitting up. "Please. My nerves are shot, I can't lie here any longer. Let me be useful. I've sat watch before, and you'll both be right here."

115

His frown deepens. His eyes are dark pools cast in shadow by the light of the moon. Finally he nods.

"Fine. Thank you. If you tire, do not hesitate to wake Ryuth."

"I won't," I reassure him, moving to settle into the spot he'd taken.

He lies down, settling in. Now I wait more. Watching the area around us while I listen to Ragnar's breathing. It doesn't take long for him to fall asleep. His breathing evens out and he stops stirring. Poor guy's been running around the desert for days looking for me. Guilt stabs me at that and another sharp pang when I look down at Olivia's sleeping profile.

She's my friend. She's been worried sick about me. Running through the desert looking for me. Am I really going to run without a word? I pause. Am I? Biting my lip I look out into the desert then back to my friend.

She'll understand. When I get back, with him. She'll forgive me. This is one of those situations where it's better to ask forgiveness than permission. The boys here aren't going to let me go back for him. They're done with him and I can't let it go. I have to know. I have to give this a chance.

So I stand and silently leave the campsite. I'll find a way to make it up to them, but first, I have to make sure my Zmaj is okay. I have to find out if there really is such a thing as fated mates. I have to know if this pull in the core of myself towards him is something real or a figment of my imagination.

Even if it means I have to face the Tribe's anger later.

19

JORMUND

*E*very part of my body hurts. Fresh blood drips from my arm. My face is swelling, the left eye is almost closed. It doesn't matter, I can't stop.

My right leg spasms, and I stumble, but manage to right myself before I fall. When I take a deep breath, I'm stopped short by blinding pain. A rib is broken, of that I'm certain. It doesn't matter, I can't stop.

Forcing myself upright through willpower alone, I move forward. My tail drags the sand, damaged as well. Blood trickles out of my mouth. It doesn't matter, I can't stop.

I have to reach her. My treasure. I have to know she is okay. I have to make her understand. *Words.* I must find the words, so she'll know. So I can make it real to her. I didn't mean harm. I would never harm her, never.

It doesn't matter that they will beat me. I will take the pain for the chance to see her. To be near her. To know that she is okay. That she will be cared for as I would care for her.

I was lost. Too lost to my bijass. Barely myself. Even now, feeling more like me than I've been in so long, parts of me

117

are hidden. The bijass is strong, calling to me, offering its sweet oblivion.

The bijass is simple. Kill, eat, sleep. Repeat.

No worry about thought. No worry about feelings. Nothing but the simplicity of primal need.

She cut through that thick, rolling fog and called to me. The brightest star, calling to my soul, pulling me from the slumber I'd retreated into. She has awoken the male I was, the male I could be again, but not without her.

Without her there is no purpose.

I force my focus to stay on the tracks. I have been trailing them for quite some time. It should be an easy enough endeavor, but the guster attack, followed by the hard fall, the kigyo I had to fight, and then the battle with the other Zmaj warriors...

The accumulation of wounds is slowing me down, making it hard to concentrate. Following a simple trail through the desert is not as easy as it should be. Every step is stabbing pain, each moment of rest is a throbbing ache. None of it is anywhere near how much my chest hurts from the loss of my treasure.

I do not know what I will do once I find them. Which I will, even if it takes me days or weeks. There are two of them, and they have not been beaten down by multiple fights as I have. I am likely to be defeated by them again even if I do reach them. I cannot give up. I will not.

What point is there in living if she is not with me? No, I must find her. No matter how long it takes me. I limp over another dune, deliberately sliding down the other side. It is faster than I can currently walk.

At the base of the dune I give myself two breaths of rest, staring up at the stars overhead. She is a gift from there. From the sky above, my treasure, she is meant to be mine. I'm certain of it. The dragon's claim is laid, and now nothing

DRAGON'S REDEMPTION

else matters. Pain is transient, she is forever. Her touch has left an indelible mark on my soul.

Inhaling gingerly, I force myself back to my feet, steeling myself for the seemingly never-ending journey to finding her. The darkness of night makes the already monotonous landscape blend even more together, the stars in the sky adding to the feeling of expansive space.

When I climb up another rise, there will be another to climb. And another. But I will not give up. I cannot give up any more than I can will myself to stop breathing. The aches and pain only make it more real that I must continue.

Head down, I start the climb up the next dune. One foot then another. When I reach the top, then I'll look for signs of my treasure. Every step the pain spikes, flashing brightly, then fading as I lift my foot again. Keep going. She's waiting.

Something pulls my attention. It cuts through the pulsing pain, the single-minded focus. Not a warning, a sense of....

A silhouette is on top of the dune I'm climbing. I frown, stopping where I stand. Is that...?

She stops too, staring back at me. My treasure. I would know those eyes anywhere, no matter the darkness lying heavy on us. Breath comes short, my hearts race, a tingling sensation races across my scales.

She came back.

Alone, in the dark, through the desert. She knows how dangerous that is, but she did it. There can be only one reason for her to have risked her life. Me. She came back for me.

Love is an aching emptiness yearning to be filled, over-riding the pain. She is the reason why I have survived all these years. She is the reason I've lived, though I didn't know it then. I live to care for her, to protect her, to shelter her. She is mine. My destiny.

She breaks the stillness before I do. Silent, she runs down

119

the expanse between us and leaps into my arms. I catch her in mid-air, wrapping her tightly, lifting her up so I can reach her lovely mouth.

Her lips seek mine as eagerly, her hands sliding into my hair as our lips meet. Yes. I deepen the kiss, tasting her, taking in her breath. She matches every touch, every caress, her desire for me clear.

Mine. She is mine.

She breaks the kiss, pulling back to look into my eyes. Moisture leaks from hers, her hands cupping my cheeks.

"You're hurt," she murmurs, taking me in.

I cup the backs of her hands with my own.

"It is fine," I say slowly, the words odd in my mouth.

She shakes her head as if to disagree, but her next words do not have to do with my physical state.

"I think I love you." She laughs, her voice thick. "I love you and I don't even know your name."

My hearts want to beat free of their cage, pounding hard enough it feels like they could break another rib. The muted colors of the night are suddenly bright and vibrant, detailed in every way. The breeze is a loud rush in my ears, my senses are alive, tingling with sensations.

She loves me. This treasure loves *me*.

I struggle to find the words. There are words, the right words, I need them. She needs to hear them. I need to express this thought that is too big to contain. Somehow, I need her to know it. Where are the words I need to say?

The fog of the bijass swells and recedes, holding its claim on the past, hiding them from me. Once I knew them. Once I had a name, that is what she asks of me. Focus, a name! What is it?

"Jormund." I offer my heart with my name.

She smiles, her eyes lighting up with a joy that mirrors my own. She leans her head against my chest, her hands

DRAGON'S REDEMPTION

wrapping around my waist. I close my eyes, resting my head on top of hers. I could stay like this forever. Everything that matters is right here in my arms.

"Jormund," she whispers against my chest.

Her soft breath wafting across my scales causes a shiver. Her skin is warm, she is warmth, a well-stoked fire that I hold in my arms. Granting me life by her very presence. The burning light calling me through time and space. She is my purpose, my reason to exist. She completes me.

"De-li-lah," I say, forcing my tongue to form the syllables of her name. It's hard. My mouth isn't used to doing more than taking in food.

She looks up, her soft fingers touching my face, tracing the lines of my jaw, running over my lips. She stretches her neck up and kisses me softly, my lower lip, my upper, retreats and nods. Patient, letting me find the words, her kindness is without bounds.

"Treasure," I offer. "Mine."

She bites her full lower lip, the lids of her eyes dropping to half, then those lush lips tremble and she nods, kissing me again, this time more fully. Insistently. Her arms tighten around me, sliding up to embrace my neck.

Passion rises but it's a side note to our coming together. We're joining in a way that is more than physical, the meeting of our lips is only a representation of what is happening between us. She is mine, offering herself to me and I give myself to her in full.

At last she breaks the kiss, the demands of air overriding our desire to not let the moment end. My hands roam over her, hers on me, and our eyes meet.

"Is there an oasis nearby?" she asks. "We need to take care of your wounds."

I look around, taking in our location and getting my bearings.

MIRANDA MARTIN

"Not... far."

She nods. It is not close, but it is a distance we can travel easily enough. I wrap an arm around her waist and flare my wings out, setting out in the right direction. We go faster than we did before, now that I am not worried about how she will react to my touch. The pain is a background noise, secondary to caring for her.

"Why did you want to leave in the middle of the night?" she asks, as we move through the silent desert. "What was the emergency?"

She's using too many words too fast. I struggle to break them down, make them make sense. It takes time but her patience shines once more. When I finally figure out what she's saying I sigh. Frowning, I try to find the words I need from the murky depths of my mind.

I choose and discard different ones that do not feel right, the silence stretching between us, but my treasure only waits patiently while I struggle internally to find the way to say the thoughts I have, explain what was going on in my mind.

"Saw... other Zmaj's...tracks," I admit.

The words are difficult, but not as difficult to find as before. Any improvement is appreciated—it helps me speak with Delilah.

"Worried that they would find me?" she asks, her voice soft.

I nod my agreement, but it was more than that. I swim in my own thoughts, searching for what I need. The words seem to slip through my fingers, there, but difficult to grasp and hold on to. How do I explain this to her? I need her to understand. This can't be between us. It has to be… known. Clear.

The throbbing pains of my body are making finding the words even harder. Every time I start to grasp one a new pain or an old one flashes hot, exploding the concept before I

DRAGON'S REDEMPTION

can use it. I don't give up. As with any fight, it's often about persevering long enough to win.

At last I find the right ones. Or at least ones that say what I mean.

"Take... you."

She nods, frowning.

"They don't understand that you aren't a bad person," she explains. "They only know that you... took me. Like you feared they would take me back."

So many words. Frowning, pressing past the pain, I play them over and over until at last the meaning becomes clear. When it does it's no surprise what they mean.

"I... understand," I say gravely. "You... treasure."

She smiles, shaking her head.

"I don't know about that."

I tighten my hold. The words are coming easier. It reminds me of the time I was poisoned and had to lie in my cave for many days. When I went to move again my muscles were slow to respond, their disuse giving way to a slackness. An unwillingness to react and move. Speech would seem to be the same. I haven't spoken in so long but now, remembering it, the ability is coming back.

I had no idea how much I missed this. Missed having another to share my thoughts with, to listen to, to hear their ideas.

"I do," I respond confidently.

She laughs softly shaking her head. The sound is so beautiful. I want her to always be laughing and smiling. Happy.

"Oh—is that the oasis?" she asks, pointing.

I follow her finger to the outline of trees not too far in the distance.

"Yes," I murmur, increasing my speed.

Now that it is so close, water sounds wonderful. This particular oasis is not the largest, which is good for our

MIRANDA MARTIN

needs. It is simple enough to do a quick scan, to ensure that there are no predators waiting under cover. After doing a quick circuit of the sparse tree line, I take us inside to the water itself.

The starlight glistens off the clear pool in an invitation I do not want to refuse. Delilah steps away from me, reaching for her clothing. My heartbeat increases, my eyes glued to her as she takes off her shirt, there's a scrap of cloth still covering the smooth mounds rising from her chest. My cock stiffens at the sight, it's exotic. Different.

She takes off her pants. Then the small scraps of clothing covering her breasts and softness between her legs. Leaving her completely bare in the gentle light of the stars.

I stare, my starving eyes not knowing where to look first. The high curves of her breasts are tipped with pretty dark nipples, giving way to the delicate curve of her waist and the generous roundness of her hips. Her legs are equally luscious, curved thighs leading to pretty calves and slender ankles.

She is different from Zmaj females, her tenderness unprotected. My cock fights my loincloth as I look at her beauty. I want to touch her, taste her, everywhere. When I finally look up to her face, it's to find her own looking back at me with just as much heat.

"Come," she whispers hoarsely, stepping closer. "We need to clean you off..."

Her soft fingers reach under the waistband of my only covering, sliding it down my hips and off my body. She stares at what she's exposed as she lowers herself down on her knees in front of me, reaching for my boots.

But she does not touch me as she divests me of my shoes and rises back to her feet. Taking my hand, she leads me into the water. The gentle warmth of it laps against my skin, my feet sink into the soft sand.

DRAGON'S REDEMPTION

She takes us in up to her chest and up to my waist, her eyes scanning my body for the various cuts and bruises I've acquired over the past few days.

She makes a sound of sympathy, cupping water with her hands and pouring it carefully over my skin, using gentle hands to scrub at the dirt and grime that has accumulated on me. When she is satisfied that my body is clean, she pulls me down, going under the water with me to clean our hair and faces as well.

When we stand back up, I feel much better than I did before. Being clean is a big difference. Her hands continue to slide over me, this time with less purpose. They smooth over my shoulders, my arms, my chest. Down to my thighs. She wraps her arms around me once more, but then stills.

"Does it hurt?" she asks, looking up concern in her eyes.

I shake my head. Any pain is not worth mentioning. Not when I want her hands on me so badly. She bites her lip, still hesitating.

Reaching down to cup the bare, slick curves of her bottom, I pick her up, bringing her face up to my own. I hiss as her soft cleft slides over my throbbing cock.

The kiss is not as soft and gentle as I originally intended. Squeezing her backside, I slide my tongue into her mouth, absorbing her taste.

The way her hard nipples rub against my chest. The gentle rocking of her hips against me.

My cock is already leaking in anticipation, so hard that every glancing touch feels almost like too much. And not enough.

I break the kiss, resting my forehead against Delilah's. Her breathing is as fast as my own.

"Delilah... I want... inside."

She reaches down, taking my erection in her soft palm. I groan, my eyes glued to the way her hand moves on me. Up and down. Just hard enough to make things worse. Her hand looks so soft, so small against my cock.

"Maybe... go slow?" Delilah murmurs, clearly noticing the same.

I nod.

"Yes."

I will not hurt her. Which means I need to make sure she is very ready for me. Turning in the water, I walk us toward the bank, laying her down on the soft sand.

She watches me, raising her arms in invitation. I settle down on top of her, kissing her deeply, my hands caressing her soft curves. Her skin is so silky under my hands. So smooth.

Leaving her lips, I kiss my way down her slender throat, down to the perfect curves of her breasts.

Her breath catches, her hands sliding into my hair as I lay small, suckling kisses along them, stopping to pay special attention to the tight points of her nipples. Her fingers clench in my hair as I suck and lick, enjoying her reaction.

When her legs are moving underneath me in reaction, I continue my journey down. Across her smooth stomach. Down to that soft place between her legs. I push her thighs apart and bury my face against her.

"Jormund!" she cries out.

Her hands clench in my hair as I lick at her, tasting her desire. I quickly find the small nub at the top of her cleft that makes her clench in reaction.

Mmm.

I lick and suck at it, carefully sliding a finger into her tight little entrance below. I will have to work to fit my cock inside.

Listening to her cries increase in volume, I hold her down and suck harder. Until her body arches against the sand and she clenches down on my finger.

DRAGON'S REDEMPTION

Keeping my mouth on her, I slide another in, deliberately stretching her. I only lift my face when she relaxes onto the sand once more, her body covered in a sheen of sweat.

I rise up, taking in her pleasure-flushed face, her half-closed eyes. Feeling a sense of true satisfaction. I gave her this pleasure.

I lean down and kiss her swollen lips, my hand going to the base of my cock. I slip the head into her wet opening, hissing at the feel of her heat surrounding even that much of me.

Despite how ready she is, she is still very tight around me. I will have to go slow.

Reaching between us, I rub her as I start to thrust inside, small, controlled movements to help make room for me. She makes small sounds as I work myself in, but they aren't pained ones.

Breaking the kiss, I prop myself up on my elbows so I can see her face. I push in that last inch, the last ridge at the base of my cock pressing into her nub. Her neck arches back, her eyes opening as she gasps in response.

"Yes?" I ask, smoothing her hair back from her damp face.

She smiles.

"Yes."

I kiss her softly, pulling out carefully. And pushing back in.

She bites her lip, her eyes closing once more at the sensations. I look down between us as I continue, watching my now-wet length slide back in. And out.

I grit my teeth, trying to last, feeling that rising heat at the base of my spine that signals the end is near. But I need to make sure this is pleasurable for Delilah.

So I continue to go slow, angling her hips so the ridges along my length hit her where it will do the most good. My eyes caress her body, drinking in the feminine curves, the gorgeous skin.

I love the expression on her face as her climax draws near. Her brows knit slightly, her lips part slightly, the flush in her cheeks deepening. The low moan that she makes this time sends a shiver down my spine.

Coupled with the way her nails dig into my back and how tightly she clamps down on my length...

There is no stopping my climax.

Gritting my teeth, I slide in as far as I can go, the orgasm rushing through me in a wave of pleasure that is so sharp it is almost pain. One that I would gladly endure over and over again.

My arms are trembling when I open my eyes again. The first thing I see is Delilah's lovely face. My hearts fill with a love so great I wonder how it can be contained. I do not deserve this treasure, but I refuse to ever part with her.

20

DELILAH

I'm a limp noodle. In the best way possible. Everything tingles, from my head to my toes.

I didn't know what to expect from Jormund. I certainly wasn't ready to have my mind blown like this.

Lying still, I keep my eyes closed until the sensations slowly recede and a level of normal awareness returns. When I open my eyes, Jormund's are there, waiting. The expression in his is soft and wondering. I smile, reaching up to cup his cheek.

Suddenly, I still when I feel something else. I know he came. I felt it, but there's definitely an erection pressing against me.

My eyes widen as I remember a very key part of Zmaj male anatomy. They have two penises. Jormund leans down to kiss me, his lips soft and gentle as he pulls out his spent cock and the still hard one nudges me.

Oh man. I'm not sure if I have another time in me. Jormund pulls back, leaning in to nuzzle at my ear.

"I want... behind," he whispers, his hot breath brushing against the sensitive skin.

I shiver at the gentle touch. Okay. Maybe I do. I nod.

Smiling, he kisses me once more before sliding off and to the side. I shift to my side as he settles in behind me. He trails kisses down my spine, then bends my top leg and pulls it up, setting his hips against mine.

Nuzzling the side of my neck, he slowly sinks inside me once more. I close my eyes, biting my lip as already sensitized nerve endings fire up. Oh. Oh wow.

There's no way I could have taken him at all if he hadn't spent so much time getting me ready. Even now, I feel beyond full, but in a way that only makes everything feel so damn good.

This time, he moves with long, smooth strokes that gently stoke the fire. I sigh, resting my head on his bicep as I let the sensations wash over me. The ridge on his erection hits... just right.

His hand smooths across my breasts, squeezing and cupping, the touch helping me draw closer to that razor-sharp edge once more. I gasp when that hand skates down my front, clever fingers finding my clitoris as he eases back into me. That's it.

This time—God, the third time? —the orgasm comes in rocking waves. Not as all-consuming as the first one, but... nice. Almost comforting.

Jormund buries his face against the back of my neck, his hand closing over my hip as he follows me over the edge, his muscles tense with his release. A wave of love flows through me. Even in this, he puts me first.

He's considerate of my needs, my feelings. He pulls me in close, kissing my cheek. Hugging me securely. I could lie here in his arms forever.

My life has always been taking care of everyone else. I'm generally pretty self-sufficient, barring the last few days. Caring for others has been my life ever since I can remem-

DRAGON'S REDEMPTION

ber. Losing my father before I even had memories of him and my mom being unable to deal with his loss left me to raise my siblings.

Yet I've been lonely. The empty ache, the need for someone to care for me, not only in a friends or family way. Someone who puts me first, above all others. Someone to treasure me. It's been a missing piece of my life.

I can't give up who I am. I'm a caregiver. I'm self-aware enough to know this about myself. I'm good at it and it does bring me great joy.

But I have needs too. Physical and emotional. Needs that I've denied for too long. Maybe... maybe I can take care of everyone else... and be taken care of myself as well.

Maybe they aren't mutually exclusive. I can have love. Maybe I don't need to choose one or the other.

"Delilah... thank you," Jormund whispers in my ear, holding me tight against his cool body.

"Hmm?" I turn in his arms so I can see his face. "Shouldn't I be saying that?" I tease.

My smile fades at the serious expression on his face. A storm of emotions dances in his eyes, plays out across his face. His mouth works, struggling to form words, but the sharp intelligence in his eyes cannot be denied.

"I... alone, long, time." He frowns. "Find you..."

He pauses, eyes boring into me, almost begging me to understand. I touch his face, my chest swelling with emotions, tears forming in my eyes. I nod my understanding. He continues.

"Only reason," he swallows, shaking his head, striving. "Lived, survived, is you. Meant for you."

My heart breaks, shattering to pieces. His words are magical, poetic in their brokenness, though they seem to be coming out easier now.

"Jormund..." I prop myself up on his chest, scanning his

beautiful face. "I'm so glad you found me. I thought... maybe I'd be taking care of everyone else and their families for the rest of my life you know? That I wouldn't ever have the chance to have my own."

He covers my hand with his own, settling his arm around my waist.

"I... care... you," he says, his brow furrowing as he finds the words. "I love you."

I duck my head, tucking it in against his neck, overwhelmed with emotion. We stay like this for a while, letting time slide pass without giving it our attention. Consumed in each other. I soak in the solidness of him, the joy in finding someone I want to spend my life with.

Eventually, real life starts to sink in as the suns crest the horizon and their first hot rays stretch to find us entwined with each other.

I lift my head so I can see Jormund's face again. He opens his eyes, looking back at me questioningly.

"Jormund... what now?" I ask, biting my lip. "I left in secret, while they were asleep."

He nods an understanding.

"Go? With me? Away?" he offers, a sweet, imploring string of words.

I could, but then how could I not see them again? Leave behind the Tribe that has become my family? Never see the babies? Never see the woman that Zoe becomes? The warriors that the twins will be? My chest aches at the thought.

"Jormund... I care for them. The Tribe, my Tribe. I don't want to leave my friends, people I love. And there's the practicality of life too—it's a lot easier to survive out here in a group. Together." I smooth a hand down his arm, taking in his tense face. "I want you to come back with me to the Tribe."

He frowns and deep in those rich eyes I see his concerns before he ever tries to give voice to them. Right, Delilah, how about I come back with you and say hi to the people who beat the shit out of me?

They won't, I 'm sure. I can make them understand, they have to. Somehow. I can't quit thinking that they accepted Ryuth, then they can accept Jormund. I know they will, given a chance to get to know him. To see in him what I do.

Jormund sighs, shaking his head. "I not welcome."

"You... got off on the wrong foot." Okay, an understatement, but still. "Once they get to know you, they'll like you as much as I do."

The love on his face is undeniable. He kisses my nose, my forehead, and then softly my lips. His hands trail up and down my bare body as he buys time to figure out the words or distracts me, either way it's nice and I'm not complaining.

"Maybe," he says at last. "I not know right."

"Please? Can we at least try?" I implore.

I'm torn between my feelings for him and those for the Tribe. I can't choose between them! I can't imagine living anywhere but with the Tribe. Everyone there is such an integral part of my life now. Yet I also can't imagine returning to my life there without him. The empty ache that had become my constant companion. The jealousy of seeing all my friends with their mates, the joy they took in each other. The love they had and I was denied until him.

He sighs, cupping my face in his hands. His brow furrows deeply.

"I try," he concedes.

I pepper his face with kisses. Warmth suffuses my chest and core as run my hands over him in excitement. Maybe I can have my cake and eat it too?

Sure I'm being greedy but how can I not be? He's perfect,

MIRANDA MARTIN

I know what I feel for him is real but what I feel for the Tribe is real too. How can I not strive to have it all?

"We'll figure it out. You'll see," I reassure him, leaping to my feet.

I can't help noticing the way his eyes drink me in, watching my breasts bounce, the shake of my ass. Any other person I'd feel embarrassed but the way he looks at me, it's sexy. The burning desire in his eyes is only confirmed by the stirring of his cock.

"Seriously?" I ask, arching an eyebrow as I start at his stiffening member.

He grins. "You, beautiful."

He's not apologetic in the least, and I don't want him to be. The low ache and burn deep in my core are ready for him too.

"Screw it," I say, stepping over him and planting my feet on either side.

His eyes widen as his member jumps to full attention. I squat, reaching between my legs to grasp his cock and guide it into my waiting channel.

It doesn't take long to have him fully seated inside, and then I take control. Rising and falling onto his cock, impaling myself freshly over and over. There is an edge of celebration to the sex this time. I'm taking charge, claiming my life as my own while still giving to those I love.

The excitement charges the sensations, and we race to a climax together in short moments. He grunts and hisses with each thrust in, and I'm panting heavily as that sweet edge swells then overwhelms me, carrying me off the cliff into the throes of another full orgasm.

I'm left shaking and weak. Legs too exhausted to hold me up, I collapse on his chest, thrilling to the sensation of his double hearts racing. They're pounding so hard it vibrates against me, accenting the aftershocks of my orgasm.

DRAGON'S REDEMPTION

When our breathing slows to something resembling normal, and my muscles quit quivering at last, I force myself upright and roll off of him. Lying on my back in the soft sand, I laugh. He rises up onto an elbow, fingers lightly tracing circles along my stomach.

"Delilah," he says softly.

"Yes?" I ask.

He shakes his head, blinking rapidly.

"Delilah, treasure," he says, and my cheeks warm.

In some strange way that single word makes me feel claimed, protected, owned in the best possible way because it's not making me less it's making him mine. It grows me, makes me more, makes us more.

Smiling I leap to my feet and take his hand, pulling for him to get to his feet. He groans and resists lightly, teasingly.

"Come on!" I encourage him. "We have to go, I want to make this work!"

He rises to a sitting position, his frown deepening as he looks past me towards where I think the Tribe is located.

"Try because..." he frowns searching for the words, "love... you," he says, a little grumpy.

"So noted," I say with a smile. "Come on—let's get dressed."

I keep my fingers crossed as we pull on our clothes. This has to work out. It just does.

21

DELILAH

We stare at each other, fully clothed, but suddenly reluctant to leave. The moment between us, this coming together, is more than physical. My hands resting in his look tiny compared to his much bigger ones. We don't speak, neither of us apparently wanting to break the moment. It's heavy with anticipation.

Will they accept him? Will they try to beat him again?

This time I won't stand by. Now, at long last, I know. My head and heart are clear. We are meant to be together, and he's coming back, for me. His treasure.

"Treasure," he says softly as if reading my mind.

My smile blossoms until my jaw hurts, it's so wide. His hands grip mine tighter as he looks down, staring at them. Slowly he raises my right hand to his lips, lightly kissing the back of it, then raising the left and doing the same.

"We… should go," I say, hesitating to say the words, not wanting to break this but torn by what I know is right.

The Tribe needs me, and they're going to learn to need him too. Damn it. I don't care what they want to think, I'm the one who was kidnapped. They can get over themselves!

DRAGON'S REDEMPTION

Jormund nods, turning and looping his one good arm around my waist.

As his arm encloses my body, warmth suffuses me. It reaches depths more than just my body, reaching deep in, as if this physical connection is but a representation of our heart connection. The connection that really matters. The one between *us*.

Certainty swells along behind the warmth. Certainty of our future, that together we'll work through whatever problems come our way. Maybe no one really gets their happily ever after the way I used to dream of it. Maybe the *real* happily ever after is having someone at your side when things get tough. Someone you know you can count on, who will never let you down.

I've found my someone.

Traveling back with his help is a lot easier. Mostly because Jormund does the work, lifting me up so we can skim across the sand rather than sinking in with every step. Luckily, my trail is pretty damn clear.

Jormund glances down as we travel, his face and eyes blatant with curiosity. It's easy to read him, now that I've gotten to know him better. He has a question he doesn't know how to put it into words. I wait, patient, his language skills are coming back as he emerges from the bijass. I'm sure soon he'll be able to talk fluently again. He's already better than he was.

"Where?" he asks at last.

"Where?" I respond, trying to understand what it is he wants to know.

Where... the Tribe? Home? Oh! The ship? He's never seen a human before, he must want to know where I came from. How do I explain this to him?

I know that the Zmaj know about space travel. We've figured out that there used to be an entire galactic trade

MIRANDA MARTIN

system here that Tajss was key to, and some of us at least suspect the Devastation was because of it, though none of us know how or why.

Hmm...

"Space?" I ask and point to the sky above us.

He looks up, his eyes widening, then understanding dawns in his eyes and he nods.

"Space..." he says, frowning deeper and looking up at the sky over our heads. "Ship?"

Smiling I nod.

"Yes!" I say excitedly.

"How long?" he asks.

"All my life," I respond.

"All?" his eyes widen with surprise. I nod. "No, ground, sky, all?"

"Yes," I agree. "Until we crashed here, I never knew the sky above or the feel of ground below my feet. Well, real ground. We had parks and such that gave us the illusion of being on ground. The ceilings of the ship were also designed to mimic the sky, so it felt like we were on a planet but no, I never was before here."

"Never ground..." he trails off, wonder in his voice. We travel a ways while he considers what I've told him, and I remain silent, letting him work it out in his own way. "Was... goal?"

Goal? What does he... oh, I get it.

"We were traveling to a far distant planet, one that was being prepared for us."

The ship was carrying us to ultimately deposit us on a different planet. We were going to colonize it. Well, technically not *us*, but our descendants. The journey from Earth to this other planet was too long for one generation to make it. All of the humans who live here on Tajss now were born on

138

DRAGON'S REDEMPTION

that ship. If we hadn't crashed here, we would have died on that ship.

He shakes his head, flaring his wings as we rise to the top of another dune.

"Unnatural to live, die without sky," he says in one of the most complex sentences he's given me yet, a sense of pride swells in my chest as he speaks. I'm pulling him out of his lost state. Me. He's coming back for me. "Without land."

He nods and half gestures around with his wounded arm. I shrug.

"Maybe. Truthfully, the expanse of the sky, the desert... it took some adjusting to at first. I was used to the familiar corridors and rooms of the ship. I knew where everything was. There weren't any surprises hiding behind a corner and definitely not anything that would try to eat me."

He chuckles, glancing down.

"Tajss dangerous," nodding as his face turns serious. "I protect you."

I smile, heart speeding up, cheeks flushing warm.

"Yes. There's no arguing that," I agree, certain of it.

The warm breeze wafts across us as we keep traveling, following the obvious tracks I left on my journey to him. His eyes never stop scanning, watching everything, aware of it all in ways I can only imagine. His protection is a shield, but more than anything, there's a sense of completion. That empty ache I've felt watching my friends with their mates is gone.

I can't say it or think it enough. I've found mine. He's found me. Either way, potato, po-tah-to.

"How spend days?" he asks.

His words are smoother, less broken, if still not complete sentences. While he does seem to be thinking through to figure out how to say his thoughts, he's getting faster. I would never know that he wasn't speaking at all a couple of days ago. It's kind of amazing to think about.

"Well, I was an engineer. So that took up my days during the week at least."

"Engineer?" he asks, repeating it slowly.

"Yes. It's someone who... builds things. Though, in my case, it was usually more maintenance than anything. I was in charge of the heating and cooling in one sector of the ship. So I made sure all the ducts, vents, fans, and so on were in good working order."

He nods, brow furrowing as he thinks that through.

"Night?" he prods. "Other… males?"

That makes me laugh.

"Not really," I admit. "I mean, I dated, but there was nobody serious. I'd hang out with friends, cooking, and watching the entertainment we had from Earth."

"Earth?" he asks.

"Yeah," I say, nostalgia sweeping over me. "Earth was our home planet, where we came from."

"Home?" he asks.

"Sort of? I was never there, heck, not even my parents ever saw it. It's the planet our species came from, but none of us here are really from there. We're from the ship. It's all we ever knew, and all we ever would know."

"Strange," he says.

"Not knowing my home planet?" I ask.

He shakes his head emphatically. "No, males, yours. Stupid."

"Huh?" I ask, head tilting in confusion.

"Stupid. You treasure. They miss chance, have treasure. I glad."

I roll my eyes, but I can't deny the warmth in my chest at the cheesy line.

"What about you? What did you do...before?"

DRAGON'S REDEMPTION

He frowns, his hold on me tightening.

"I was... soldier," he says slowly, his frown deepening. "I remember…"

His eyes are troubled and he's holding me tighter. It's easy to see the pain written so clearly on his face. A shiver runs through his body.

"It's okay," I say softly, laying my fingers on his face. "Don't push it. Let it be."

He shakes his head, swallowing hard.

"Must," he hisses, turmoil burning in his eyes.

He shudders, closes his eyes, and comes to a stop. I can feel his hearts pounding where I rest against him. If he was human, I have no doubt he'd be pouring sweat, but Zmaj don't sweat. Turning into him I cup his face in my hands, rising onto my toes I kiss his tight lips.

"Jormund," I whisper, peppering his lips with mine. "It's okay." His eyes open and his face softens staring into mine. "I'm here."

His wings rustle and his tail shifts from side to side faster, but he nods. Some of the tension drops out of his face.

"War," he says, his frown deepening.

"You were in the war?" I prod and he nods. "Soldier?"

"Yes," he nods.

I can't imagine war, really. We didn't know war on the ship, of course. There were vids about it, old stories about men going to war, but I was never interested in them. The history courses I took mention that they used to happen, but history was never my thing, and I really didn't care. It sounded awful, and that's all I ever needed to know.

Seeing the pain in his eyes makes it clear I was right. It must have been awful to cause him so much pain.

"Can't remember," he says, his wings open and closing as he shakes his head.

"It's fine," I tell him, "you don't have to. Let it be."

He squeezes me with his good arm, sighing, and then leans in to kiss me. His kiss is insistent, needy, almost too rough. His cock stiffens between us, pressing hard against my stomach, digging in uncomfortably for me, and I would assume it's not comfortable for him either.

His mouth claims mine, his squeeze tightens until it's hard to breathe. I pull back from his lips.

"Jormund," I exhale finding it difficult to take my next breath in. "Too… tight."

He stops instantly, relaxing his grip. "Sorry," he says, eyes scanning me up and down. "Okay?"

"Yeah, I'm fine," I say, not pulling back from him but glad to be able to breathe easier. "Were you… hurt?" I ask, trying to find the right way to ask what I want to know. His pain is palpable—I can feel it in him. I want to understand, to help him feel better. I don't want him to carry this pain. Not alone at least. Somehow, I want to shoulder this burden for him.

He nods slowly. Thoughtfully. His head tilts to one side as he stares out across the empty desert around us, but he's obviously not seeing the here and now. A sense of helplessness rises in me as I watch. There is nothing I can really do that will help, so I do the one thing I can offer right now. I remain silent, but run my hands over his face, down his neck, and across his muscled shoulders. I massage his shoulders, run my fingers around the corded muscle, down to his wings, back up, down to his chest and return to his face.

It's the only thing I can think of to anchor him here with me while he faces the demons of his past. I only hope it's enough.

2 2

JORMUND

*E*xplosions make my ears ring. I can't hear. Sand and dirt cloud the air. Can't see.

Where are my men?

Her touch pulls me, keeps me here while I'm there too.

The red fog of the bijass soars, covering the now with the past that it has hidden so long. It hurts. My chest aches, muscles feel weak, confusion swirls.

Am I here? Am I there?

My men. Must find my men. I open my mouth to yell for them, but dust and sand fill it, cutting off the sounds before I can make them. Another explosion, but I'm already deafened.

Lights flash around me. Can't see. Can't escape.

The light is blocked out. I look up... a ship. A massive ship with dozens of smaller ones buzzing around it like sand gnats to manure. They're firing, firing down on us, but that's not all, the Invaders are marching.

We're cut off. The comm in my ears screeches, loud enough to cut through the ringing. We're falling back. Fall back. That's the order.

Yelling, I call the retreat. I'm not the leader of my squad, but I don't see him.

There, Tivann. My friend, my brother in arms, he's running at me, eyes wide. The Invaders are too close, they're right behind him. One of their blue bolts strikes him in the back. He roars in surprise and pain, whipping around to face them.

Racing, leaping over the craters left by the explosions I rush to him. I reach his side at the same time the blue Invaders close with us. Their four arms and chitinous armor difficult to fight, but we'll stand together.

They force us back. My blade slides along the armor, searching for purchase. Often as not I'm blocked by the monster's two swords. He continues firing his two guns with the lower arms while fighting me at the same time.

We're losing. *I'm* losing.

I back into something as I retreat before my enemy. Barely glancing back, I see it's another of my troop. A dozen of us have found each other. We put our backs to each other, forming a circle as we're surrounded…

"Jormund," her sweet voice cuts through the noise. She's calling me. She needs me. "Jormund, come to me, please."

I must answer her call. She needs me. She is all that matters.

The scene fades. I don't know how this ends, but some sense tells me it's not good. This memory fades, becoming dim, the fog of the bijass reclaiming what belongs to it.

Her touch. Fingers running across my shoulder, rising to cup my face. My eyes clear, and she is there, before me. Smooth, dark skin perfectly illuminated by the sinking sun's light. Her full, plush lips tremble and her eyes sparkle like stars.

I pull her closer, lifting up with my good arm around her waist, and her lips meet mine. I lose myself once more but

DRAGON'S REDEMPTION

this time it's in her. The simple, luscious sensation of her lips on mine. Her body molding to me. Everything I've never dared dream, no matter what I've lost in the past, it was the journey that led me to her.

Let the past burn. She is here. She is now.

"Wow," she exhales when at last I break the kiss. I smile, staring into her beautiful eyes. "Are you okay?"

Instinctively I almost answer her instantly, but she deserves better than instinct. Looking at myself I consider the question. Am I okay?

The pain is there. An empty aching... something. Something I can't recall. Some part of me still shies from it but does it matter? How can anything be so bad?

"I…" I start to answer but then the word isn't there that says what I want to say. Frowning I search my mind for it, knowing I know it. Frustration burns hot but then it's here. "Fine. I'll be fine."

She smiles and nods, but doesn't prod.

"Good."

"Move on," I say, and she nods her agreement, turning into me and wrapping an arm around my waist.

We continue our travel in a silence that is now comfortable. An acquired certainty, I'm no longer worried I will say the wrong thing, at least as much as I was. Words are coming easier.

As we travel my thoughts drift around her and us and the future. The possibilities of what might be. I'm still concerned about the males I took her from but that will be handled when it comes time to handle it. You can't count your epis before you harvest it. You never know what will happen along the way.

If they reject me outright, I will fight them if I must. No matter what I will not let them take her from me, not again. I only did it last time because she asked me to stop. I did it for her. This time, I know she will not make me stop. She will not choose to go with them. She has come to realize for herself we are meant to be together.

Together. No longer alone.

My hearts race as more possible futures reel out. A calm, peacefulness washes through me, and the bijass retreats in the face of it. Somehow, I feel more me than since I can remember. I'm not an animal, surviving on instinct alone. I'm a male. A powerful, strong warrior who will dominate whatever I must to protect my treasure.

Dim ideas, not clear images or memories, but the concept of what came before slowly reveals itself in my thoughts. On some level I remember the war. The war that started the end. The end of everything we knew. The loss of all.

The pain of it is such that still I shy away. There is something there I don't want to remember. Some old pain that doesn't matter in the now.

Pushing it aside, I keep us moving. Climbing another of the endless dunes of Tajss, doing my best to ignore the throbbing pains of my body, I stumble to a stop. The males I took her from stand on the dune opposite a few spans away.

They stare in astonishment and as one they draw their lochabers, racing towards us.

23

DELILAH

When Jormund stops I'm half-asleep, leaning most of my weight against him. It's been two days since I've slept and longer than that since I've had a full night's sleep. The peacefulness of our journey was lulling.

His grip around my waist tightens, pulling me closer, and he hisses softly. Following the line of his gaze I see Ragnar and Ryuth running full tilt down the next dune with Olivia not far behind. They have their lochabers drawn leaving no doubts as to their intention.

Jormund looks down at me, and then he lets go and steps forward, reaching with his one good arm for his own lochaber.

"No," I say, grabbing his arm and pulling him back.

He stops, albeit reluctantly, looking over his shoulder.

"Must," he says.

"No," I say. "Not like this. There has to be a better way."

His eyes rest on my hand, staring. His bulging muscles thrum with vibrant energy under my fingers. Slowly he looks up and meets my eyes.

"Protect you," he says. "My treasure."

MIRANDA MARTIN

Warmth suffuses my chest and the fire of desire in my core flames. The way he says that is a claiming and not like anything I've ever experienced. I've heard the other males saying the same of their mates, but have never understood it, not like this. It's a simple statement, almost cliché when it comes to the Zmaj, but then I was never the receiver. Trembling I run my fingers up his arms to his face.

"I love you," I whisper, mouth dry, heart racing. "Let me do this."

It's easy to see, his thoughts are written clearly on his face. His instinct to protect, the primal part of his brain that he's only now gaining control over demanding he fight. His eyes narrow, mouth a hard line, but slowly the man that I love keeps control. He nods, a sharp gesture.

I step in front of him, blocking Ragnar and Ryuth's access. The race up the dune, weapons ready, anger written across their faces. It doesn't matter that they're angry, they don't understand. Now it's on me to make them. They intend him harm, but I'll protect him with my body if I have to.

"Get out of the way, Delilah!" Ragnar growls as he and Ryuth race towards us.

"Does he think he can just do this again with no repercussions?" Ryuth asks, incredulously.

"No!" I yell, holding up a hand.

They don't stop their mad dash, rushing forward, the rising suns glinting off the steel of their lochaber. Jormund throws his one good arm in front of me, trying to force me behind him but I grab onto his arm and spin around it so that I remain between him and them. "He isn't kidnapping me! I went back to find him!"

Ragnar comes to a step, lochaber held at the ready in front of him. His brother, Ryuth skids to a halt next to him. Olivia huffs her way up from behind but isn't here yet.

"Stop trying to protect him!" Ragnar growls.

DRAGON'S REDEMPTION

"It's the truth!" I retort.

"Wait!" Olivia calls out, red in the face and breathing heavy as she finally reaches us. She lays a hand on her mate's arm, holding him back. "Why don't we listen to what they have to say?"

Ragnar looks down at Olivia. She gives him back look for look. Sighing, he looks at Ryuth, who looks irritated and angry, but if anyone ought to understand, it's him. He was captured by the Zzlo and tortured until he was also lost in the bijass. He came back, and so has Jormund.

A Zmaj is a Zmaj, no matter their differences, they're all bound by an internal code of honor. The Tribe didn't get along with the Zmaj of the City but now we have open trade, and all work together for survival. All I have to do is navigate the waters of three alpha males' primal instincts. Piece of cake, right? Except there is no cake on Tajss.

"Fine," Ragnar bites out turning to Jormund. "Who are you? Why should we listen to anything you have to say?"

"He—" I start but Jormund cuts me off with a staying hand on my shoulder.

Looking over my shoulder he barely nods and a slight smile forms on his face. My belly flutters as I snap my mouth shut. Nodding I step to one side as he steps up beside me. If he wants to speak for himself, I should let him.

"Jormund," he says, motioning to himself with one hand.

Ragnar glares but Ryuth's expression softens as if he at least recognizes something in Jormund. As well he should, he was in the same boat not that long ago. Jormund frowns and it's easy to see he's searching for the right words to say.

"Understand," he says, patting his chest to indicate he means himself. "I take Delilah." He glances to me. "My treasure. My mate."

"Why steal her?" Ragnar asks, but he lowers his lochaber, the first sign of him softening his position.

149

Jormund shakes his head, his jaw tightens, and he frowns as his brow furrows.

"Must. Had to…" he trails off, eyes clouding over. "My treasure. She is…. Meant… for me."

Ryuth twirls his lochaber around and slides it into the straps on his back. Stepping forward he holds out a hand to Jormund.

"Ryuth," he says simply.

Jormund grips the offered hand taking it by the wrist and the two men stare into each other's eyes. Tension makes the hair on my arms stand on end as I wait to see how this is going to end. It seems good, but then it could still go either way.

When they shake, I let out the breath I was holding in a loud exhale. Olivia comes over, looking me up and down.

"Are you okay?" she asks.

"Yeah," I say, voice quavering with the release of the pent-up emotions. "It's been a long few days.

"That's for sure," she says. "You scared the hell out of us. Did he take you?"

"No," I say, not taking my eyes of the three men. "I went to him."

"That was stupid," she says, placing a hand on my shoulder.

"Probably?" I say but almost ask.

I don't know if I'm thinking clearly yet.

"It was," she affirms. "But I understand. Love can do that to you."

"Love," I say, nodding. "How did I get to this point?"

"Who knows?" Olivia laughs, pulling me into an embrace and crushing me against her. "I'm glad you're okay. That's what matters most."

I return the embrace watching Jormund over her shoulder. He and Ryuth break their handshake then Ragnar steps forward and offers his hand. He says something too soft for me to hear but I see Jormund hesitate before he accepts the offered hand.

"I want to be with him," I confirm, squeezing my friend tighter.

It's an admission, a testament, and a realization all at once.

"Good," Olivia whispers back. "You deserve someone. You need someone, someone just for you."

Tears well in my eyes at her kind words. An emotional storm overcomes me. I hadn't realized how much I'd been holding in, pushing down and keeping it out of sight out of mind. Now it all hits me and I'm sobbing in her arms. I deserve this. Someone for me.

Burying my face in Olivia's shoulder I let it out. The rush, the overwhelm, the empty ache that I've ignored for so long. She holds me tight, making soft soothing sounds and rubbing my back. We've been through so much. Life's been so full of surviving the day, I'd given up hope of finding happiness beyond what the moment offered.

Jormund offers me a future. One where I'm not destined to be alone. It's a lot to take in. Even more to let out. At last the tears dry and I straighten, Olivia releasing her hold but keeping her hands on my shoulders.

"I've gotten you all wet," I say, wiping at the last of the tears.

"It's fine," she laughs. "Sometimes we need a good cry."

"Yeah," I say, shaking my head.

"Are you fine?" Jormund asks.

"Yeah," I smile, eyes blurry still with the last of the tears. "I am. Are you?"

He looks at Ragnar before saying anything. Ragnar gives a slight nod.

"Will be," he says.

"We're bringing him home," Ragnar says. "We'll let Drosdan decide if he stays or goes."

"Stays or goes?" I ask, an empty pit opening in my stomach.

"Yes," Ragnar says flatly.

"He can't go!" I yell at him. "He's my... mate!"

The word falls off my tongue like a rock into a pool. I feel it ripple through me, pinging the depths of my soul. Ragnar doesn't answer, staring back implacably. Ryuth steps closer.

"Delilah," Ryuth says. "There are rules, traditions. They must be followed. It will be okay."

"Is... fine," Jormund says.

Olivia has an arm around my shoulders, tightening her grip but I pull away from her and move to stand right under Ragnar's nose. Glaring up at him I hold up a finger and wave it in his face.

"If he goes, I go," I threaten.

Ragnar doesn't blink, silently meeting my glare.

"Delilah," Olivia says. "It will work out. Let them keep their traditions. Everything will be okay."

"It will be, or I'll be gone," I say.

No one else says a thing. The five of us stare at each other, tension rising. I shift my gaze from one to the next, waiting for one of them to crack.

"We should go," Ryuth says, looking away first.

No one else says anything but his statement breaks the moment. Silently we turn and start the journey to the Tribe's home.

My home.

Unless....

Unless they refuse Jormund. Could they? Would they? What do I do if they do? My chest aches and it's hard to breathe considering the idea they won't accept him. I said I'd

DRAGON'S REDEMPTION

leave with him but then I'd be leaving behind everything I know. All my friends, my family, the kids…

No, they have to accept him. Surely, I have enough value that they wouldn't let me go rather than letting him join us.

What do we do if they do though?

The City? They've welcomed strange Zmaj before but when the Tribe came, they refused entry. Of course that's when that douche-tool Gershom was still around. He's gone, so maybe that's an option?

"It'll be okay," Olivia murmurs, cutting through my dark thoughts. "They just don't like change. And if you say he's a good guy…"

"He is," I say.

"Then things should be fine as long as he doesn't rock the boat," she says with a bright smile.

Sighing I nod while trying to stop my heart racing and my nerves from being a jangling mess. All I can do is keep my fingers crossed and hope. The suns are fully cresting the horizon and the heat is rising but now is the perfect time to travel. There's enough light to see by and it isn't as hot as it will be when the suns are high in the sky.

We move quickly, Ragnar and Ryuth both keeping an eye on Jormund at all times. They don't try to hide that that's what they're doing either, but it doesn't seem to faze Jormund. He silently keeps pace with them, his good arm wrapped around me to help me travel across the sand.

When we crest a dune and I see the Tribe's wall and the home we've built beyond it, my heart leaps into my throat and tears form in my eyes. It feels like it's been months instead of days since I last saw it, so much has happened in the intervening time.

It's too far for me to make out details, but I see people working behind the wall, males patrolling, people in the garden. Life. I see life as I've known it. The home and life I've built since crashing here on Tajss.

Can I leave it? If I have to, can I walk away from this? For him? Surprisingly the answer is easy.

Yes.

I can't imagine a life without him. The instant I consider it, an empty ache forms in my guts, and I know that I'd be resigning myself to a half-life. A life without true joy, incomplete. Lacking the one primal thing I need, my mate.

It's only been a few days, and this is ridiculous, but I know. I've known since the moment he first called me his treasure. When he spoke, said that word, it resonated deep inside, and I knew whether I admitted it or not. I'm his, but every bit as importantly, he's mine.

Gazing up at him, my heart gallops and my stomach flutters with butterflies. He's the one. I don't necessarily believe in fate, though I know the Zmaj do in their own way, but whether it's fate or some other natural occurrence, Jormund and I are a perfect match.

The surprise on his face is obvious as he takes in all that the Tribe has done to make this our home. He glances down, smiling, but doesn't speak. Is he imagining a life there with me? I hope so, because I am with him.

As we approach the main gate there is a flurry of activity and shouts. The gates open, welcoming us home. It looks like a majority of the Tribe are gathered to greet us inside too. All my family and friends. I'm not surprised, we were due back a few days before so I'm sure they were worried.

Passing through the gate Jormund strains his neck to look all around at once.

"This is... impressive," he remarks.

I look around, seeing with his eyes. The large wall for protection, the thriving garden, all the people who've gathered around to greet us, including multiple human females.

DRAGON'S REDEMPTION

The kids break free from the adults, Elneese and Ganeese in the lead with Leia and Aeros not far behind. They're laughing and giggling as they race towards us until Elneese pushes Ganeese, causing him to stumble, Elneese pulling ahead.

"Hey, not fair!" Ganeese yells as Aeros crashes into him and the two of them fall to the ground, entangled with each other.

"Slow down!" I cry out, trying to calm their excitement before it gets out of hand.

Elneese skids to a stop in front of us, staring up at Jormund. Ganeese climbs to his feet then helps Aeros up.

"Sorry," he says.

"I'm good!" Aeros says cheerfully.

Leia walks past the two boys with barely a disdainful glance, approaching with a solemnity that is way beyond her small years.

"Who are you?" Elneese says, crossing his arms over his chest and staring up defiantly.

Ganeese runs up beside his brother and in mirror fashion duplicates the same stance, adding his own glare.

Jormund stares with his eyes wide, so still he could be made of stone. Slowly he lowers himself to a crouch before the twins. As he does, Aeros and Leia come up but stay a step behind the twins.

Jormund's mouth moves but no sound comes out but a soft hiss. A shudder causes his wings to rustle and his tail suddenly shifts from side to side.

"Children," he says at last, wonder in his voice.

"This is Jormund," I say, kneeling beside him. "He's my... friend."

"He looks dangerous," Ganeese says.

"Yup, dangerous," Elneese says. "We gonna have to beat you down?"

The twins are defiant as ever and fearless.

"Boys," Zoe says, appearing as if out of nowhere, her voice sharp. "Calm down."

She looks at me and rolls her eyes, shaking her head before turning her attention to Jormund.

"You're late," she says, matter-of-factly. "I've been waiting for you forever, what took you so long?"

Her tone might have been intimidating except for the fact that she's so small and cute, her bright blue eyes and red hair shining in the sunlight, baby horns just peeking through the soft strands.

Her announcement gives everyone pause. I know some of the children have had moments, done things that would lead you to believe they have psychic abilities, but it sets me back on my feet when I see it. Olivia steps forward and scoops up her daughter, kissing her pink cheeks.

"I missed you so much, baby."

"I missed you too, Mommy!" she cries out, wrapping her arms around her mother and promptly forgetting about Jormund.

Right back to being a normal little girl. Jormund turns to me with joy in his eyes.

"Children?" he asks.

I smile and nod as he takes my hands in his. "Yes."

"And they… human and...?"

"Zmaj," I confirm, taking his hand. "They're both."

Hope lights in his eyes and his smile widens. There isn't much time to enjoy the moment as Drosdan walks up to us. Drosdan is big, bigger than all the other Zmaj. Massive arms that look like tree trunks and a barrel chest. He scans over Jormund as he approaches, sizing him up.

Jormund sees my gaze shift to Drosdan, following it. When he sees the big Zmaj he drops my hands and turns to face him. He meets his look with a steady one of his own, his hands loose at his sides, his feet shoulder width apart. A neutral but not subservient stance.

"You are Jormund?" Drosdan greets him, no pleasantries wasted.

"Yes," Jormund agrees.

He narrows his eyes at the short response.

"You kidnapped Delilah?" he asks point blank.

I want to jump in, but I know that it's better if Jormund handles this himself. It isn't easy to pull back, but I do it. Jormund's jaw tightens and his hands twitch, but it's only an instant, and he's back in full control.

"Did not hurt her. She is treasure, my mate," he glances at me, the love in his eyes clear to any onlooker while motioning to his chest.

Drosdan nods, the tension easing slightly, but he's still frowning deeply. Is this going to work?

"We have Edicts, you must know them, accept them, live by them," Drosdan says.

"E-dicts?" Jormund asks.

Drosdan doesn't answer, waiting for something, but I don't know what. He nods sharply and waits.

"Edicts, a code the Zmaj of the Tribe live by," I try to explain.

Jormund nods without breaking eye contact with Drosdan. The tension in his muscles makes it clear he's struggling to maintain control. Drosdan isn't helping, but then it hits me. Drosdan is pushing his buttons. When I glance around, I realize that the other Zmaj have formed a circle around us, close, close enough to be a threat. They want to see if Jormund will attack them. If he will be subservient or if he will fight.

It's a subtle test, but a test none the less. The bijass makes them primal, reducing them to acting on base instincts. They become fight-or-flight and super-alpha so they're seeing how he reacts. My heart races as cold sweat pours down my spine.

I don't know how I can help him. Looking around I see friendly faces, but I know these people. They're my family and friends, to Jormund they're all strangers. All potential threats—he doesn't know them or their intentions. How will he react?

There's only one thing I can do, so I do that. I take his hand in mine, silently supporting him. When I squeeze his hand the tension in him drops away, and with it the tension among all the Zmaj. It's almost as if they have some special instinct that senses something in each other.

"What…" he pauses, frowning as he searches for the word. "… are they?"

"One," Drosdan says, his deep voice booming and echoing around us. "I am myself."

Jormund nods his understanding.

Drosdan opens his mouth to continue but a sudden whining sound drowns out any sounds he might have made. Then the air is split, and a thunderclap leaves my eardrums ringing.

"Invaders!" someone yells loud enough to be heard over the noise.

My stomach drops. Oh no.

24

JORMUND

The loud whine is ear-splitting. Instinctively, I grab Delilah with my good arm and pull her to me, protecting her with my body.

When I look up, a cold chill races through me, and the bijass rushes forward, grabbing for control. I know this. I've seen this before. It can't be happening again.

Fear.

Cold, dark, gripping hands clench onto my thoughts. I can't tell if this is real or memory. Instinctively I scoop Delilah her off her feet and run.

Shelter. Have to find shelter.

Protect her.

Can't lose her. Can't let them get us, not again.

"Jormund!" she cries out but there's no time to explain.

Words are too slow, need action. Move. Save her. No matter what it takes, save her. Can't lose her. Can't lose again.

Shouts and screams come from all around. I'm not sure what's real and what's memory. Everything is blending, mixing, confusing.

MIRANDA MARTIN

Delilah pounds her small fists against my chest. Her eyes are wide, yelling, but I can barely spare the instant to glance at her. I'm running through these other people, dodging around them to get her to safety.

The cave opening yawns large before us. It will offer safety. If I get her there, then I can fight. Digging deep, I push past the pains of my body. It protests. There is agony with each motion forward but saving her is above it all.

As the cool dark of the cave falls over us, I run up to the crowd of other females like her. Setting her down, I grip her waist, staring into her beautiful face. Etching the lines of it, the sparkle of her eyes into my mind's eye.

I know what awaits me out there. Tightness and pain grip my chest. I open my mouth to say something, anything to her but no words come out. Dim memories swirl behind the fog of the bijass. The dragon rages, roaring against what is to be.

"Jormund," she says, her fingers on my face.

I shake my head, unable to force the words out, but she knows. My heart knows she knows. I will do anything for her. Including face them.

Them.

I remember them, barely, but I know it's bad. Terrible. Death from the sky.

Whirling around I run back outside. I hear her calling my name after me, but there is no time for this. The other males race towards the gates. I glance up, and my stomach drops when I see one of the ships directly above, the massive gun glowing with bright light as it prepares to fire.

The now is overlaid with the past. Memories vie for control of reality. What is and what was confusing and jumbling.

My men are with me, we're armed, advancing on orders to take the enemy. Outnumbered, but we were the best. We would not be beaten.

DRAGON'S REDEMPTION

Until we were.

The air splits and I duck my head instinctively, though I know that it won't matter. If I'm in the range of that gun above, it's over. A crackling sound echoes off the cliff walls. I look up and I'm stunned to see an amber shield making a dome over the Tribe's home. The gun's emission breaks over it, creating a light show of dancing lightning.

A shield?

Impressive. Hope blossoms inside me beneath the swirling grip of the past and fear. If their ships are neutralized, then we can win.

"Here!" Ragnar yells, motioning for me to join him.

I run for him, his face blurring, becoming someone long gone. I blink my eyes rapidly until his face resolves into being who he is. Ragnar, not my long-lost squad mate.

"They'll drop down, we fight them beyond the wall!" he yells, pointing. "Can you fight?"

He looks at my injured arm as he asks.

"Yes," I hiss, taking my lochaber off my back with my good one and whirling it to ready with one hand.

"Good," he nods.

The big one that greeted me and was talking is shouting orders. We form into groups of three and race through the gate to greet the enemy head-on.

Groups of three.

The same as it was before. Suddenly the memories flood out of the fog of the past. I remember...

"Pay attention!" Drosdan's deep voice cuts through the fog and the memories, pulling me back to the now.

Growling, I nod and follow him and the others outside the wall. On the closest dune two ships are unloading the enemy. The ships hover over the sand, their engines creating a cloud of sand and dust that obscures vision.

As we exit the gate, our groups split up while all heading

161

MIRANDA MARTIN

towards the enemy. Force them to spread out, don't group. Keep them from being able to use their superior firepower, bring to bear their air cover.

The enemy emerges from the clouds of sand and dirt. My hearts gallop, my throat is dry, and I know these beasts. Monsters. They were there. There before the Devastation. I was held by them, tortured, locked in small cages along with my men.

Now they come for my treasure.

My pulse pounds in my ears and my limbs tingle, hands twitching with the desire to squeeze the life out of them for daring to threaten her. Roaring, I charge.

Shouts echo behind me, the other males crying out their surprise or outrage, but I don't care. I'm going to stop these monsters. I know what they are capable of, what they will do, and I won't allow it.

Drawing closer, I see their blue skin. The one I approach has yellowed eyes, scarifications on his face, and four arms. All of his body is covered in fancy armor.

"Die!" I scream, swinging the lochaber over my head, around and down, sweeping at his legs below the armor.

He tries to move, bringing his own weapon around to block mine, but he's too slow. The blood spurts out of the deep wound, then I jerk the lochaber free and it sprays across the sand. He screams in pain.

Two more close from either side. I whirl on the closest to my left, who ducks my swing and the one behind prods me with his weapon.

Pain explodes from the point of contact, my thoughts are blasted apart. I cry out in pain. Delilah's face swims through the stars dancing in my eyes, and I force my attention under control.

Tucking my head, I throw myself to one side and do a shoulder roll. My damaged arm bangs the sand hard as I do, creating a fresh burst of pain, but it is buried by the dragon inside. Fuel for its rage.

Rolling several times I come to a stop in a crouch, facing my opponents. They close cautiously, knowing I am dangerous.

Good. Let them know fear.

Grinning I hiss, tail rising up behind me, wings spreading. The one to the left hesitates, it's the opening I need.

Leaping up and forward I hold the lochaber tucked under one arm, pointed blade aimed at my enemy.

He drops to a knee, intending to roll forward but I adjust my wings and shift the lochaber. Dropping down, I drive the blade into his back. It scrapes across the steel of his armor, screeching as it looks for purchase. Then it catches.

As I fall onto it, the tip of the blade slides between the plates of his armor and into his flesh. He screams as my body weight forces the blade through him into the sand beneath.

The other slams into me, knocking the lochaber out of my hand.

We roll across the sand, each struggling to come out on top. He growls, I hiss back at him, rage growing. His beady, black pupils pour his hate into me, but it cannot match my own. His kind beat my men. Beat me. Tortured us. Showed no mercy, then left us.

They must pay. All of them must pay.

We roll off the top of the dune we're on, and the somewhat controlled tumbling becomes chaos. We bounce off of each other as gravity takes over. Hitting the ground, each other, slamming into body parts or hard earth, the wind is knocked out of me.

We land a few feet apart. I'm gasping air, trying to force it into my lungs. Every muscle screams in protest. Everything hurts. I could give up. It'd be easy, the way out. End my long existence.

No. She needs me.

The thought of Delilah drives me forward. I force myself to rise and roll to my feet. I stumble to one side, saving myself a new wound as the Invader thrusts a sword passing within inches of my ribs.

I face off against him, alone. The others are no longer in sight. There is me and this monster who would hurt my treasure. Who, for all I know, hurt my men too. He could be one of those who did.

He utters some guttural sounds, growls and clicks. Brow furrowing, I wipe my arm across my mouth, noticing the blood but not caring.

"You're going to die," I say softly.

Words come easier. I know. I remember. I am myself. Drosdan's words echo through my thoughts, but more, they resonate deeply.

He laughs. That's fine. He'll learn soon enough.

His eyes watch me as we circle one another. He feints in and I move to block but don't commit. I feint and he does the same. We dance, slowly but surely as we watch for the slip.

Sooner or later, one of us will. It's the way of battle. One instant, and it's over. The smart warrior creates that instant.

Gaining a feel for my opponent, I purposely drop my guard, leaving my wounded arm open. He can't resist the opportunity, lunging forward.

Instead of meeting him head-on, I step inside his lunge, twisting around his arm as he grabs for me. I slam my elbow onto the back of his neck at the same time swinging my tail around and slamming it into his legs.

A satisfying crunch sounds followed closely by his screams. He drops to the ground, broken. Ignoring him, I run up the dune to rejoin the rest of the battle.

25

DELILAH

"When will this ever stop?" Bailey asks.

She's trembling, surrounded by the rest of us women. We stand in a loose circle with the babies in the middle of us. The old saying of "it takes a Tribe" is true, especially here. We all contribute to the care of the babies. It's especially true when we're under attack. Again.

Outside the cave Errol, Kalessin, and Falkosh stand guard, a last stand resort for sure. Kalessin and Falkosh are so old they even look old to the eye. I have no idea how old that means they really are, but the other Zmaj consider them Elders. Considering that as far as we've been able to figure out, the Zmaj live for hundreds of years they could be dozens of decades old for all I know.

If the Invaders make it to the cave, we're in trouble. That's the summary of it. I can barely think of that, though. All I can think about is Jormund, out there, already badly hurt. Fighting to protect me.

The musky, spicy scent of his body teases through my thoughts. Grabbing me off my feet with his one good arm and running, nothing I did to resist mattered. As if I was

165

nothing until he got me to safety. The look in his eyes, on his face when he put me down and paused. The love so clearly burning through, there is no doubt he had but one thought. Protect me.

But he's hurt.

His arm was bleeding again before he left. His body covered with softly shining bruises from the beatings he's endured, all to have me. I can't imagine how much pain he must be in and now he faces the very formidable Invaders.

We don't even have a name for them. The aliens who keep showing up, keep attacking us, but never for any clear-cut purpose. They wanted the meteorite glass but that's mostly been harvested so why do they keep coming back?

"What do they want?" Penelope asks, cutting into my own line of thinking.

"I don't know," I say.

"They want what we have," Zoe says, cryptically. "They want Tajss."

All of us turn and look at her. She's not looking at any of us. Her eyes look to be focused on some distant thing only she can see, staring off into space. Sometimes she says things that make no sense. We've all noticed how she often says things she can't possibly know, but they almost always come true. When she speaks like this it's not like you're listening to a three-year-old toddler but an ancient wise woman.

The other kids cling to their mothers, but Zoe stands in front of Olivia without fear. A small smile plays on her face as if she's enjoying what she sees.

"We should fight them too," Elneese says, suddenly struggling against Mei.

Ganeese follows his brothers lead, and the two boys slip out of Mei's grip as she struggles to hold the two toddlers. Ganeese runs past, and I lunge to catch him. I barely get a

DRAGON'S REDEMPTION

grip on the edge of his pants before he's out the opening of the cave.

"Woah!" I yell.

"Let me go," he yells, whirling around. "I can fight too.

"We can fight," Elneese yells, being held by Mei. "Come on Mommy, we're big boys now, we're men!"

He slams a fist against his bare chest, holding his head up proudly.

"You'll think you're a big boy when your father gets home," Mei says sternly. "You know what he has said about you fighting."

Ganeese stops struggling against my grip the instant his father is mentioned and out of the corner of my eye I see Elneese stops too.

"I'll fight soon," Pachua says calmly from Maeve's arms. "But I'm not big like my daddy yet. Soon though, right Mommy?"

"Yes, my sweet boy," Maeve says, kissing the top of his head. "You're growing up fast."

Ganeese walks back to his mother, arms crossed over his broadening chest with a scowl on his face.

"I'm ready," he humphs. "I'd show those monsters what for."

"Soon enough," Mei says, kneeling in front of him and his brother. "But what does your daddy say?"

The twins look at each other, perfect mirror opposites. Watching them you can almost see the way they communicate to one another without words, as if they have their own language only they understand.

"A warrior fights smart," they say in unison.

"Right," Mei agrees.

"Ugh," Ganeese rolls his eyes.

"Zoe!" Olivia yells and we all turn to her.

Zoe is gone. She was there, only a moment ago she was right there.

I spin on my heel to look for her in one fast glance around, but there isn't a sign of her. Panic makes Olivia's voice shrill as she calls for her daughter again.

All my fears for Jormund are overwritten by the cold ball of ice in my guts.

Zoe is gone.

26

JORMUND

There are too many of them. They're everywhere, and they keep coming. The past pushes into my thoughts, clouding the world in front of me with the world that was. The world where I lost.

Delilah. The scent of her anchors me, calls me to the now. The feel of her in my arms, the light in her eyes, all keep dragging me out of the past.

"They're heading for the wall!" one of the males yells, one of them I don't know.

He's big but not as big as Drosdan. He motions towards the wall, and it's easy to see the concern. There are a dozen of them heading for it, while another dozen form a line blocking us from reaching them.

Delilah!

The dragon roars to life, molten fire searing through my veins, and I roar. Unable to contain the rage.

Two of the monsters before me step back, shaken by what they see. Fear blossoms in their eyes like a delicate flower exposing itself to the harsh suns. Wielding my recovered lochaber one handed, I attack with renewed vigor.

I will stop them.

A red filter covers my vision and then everything is motion and sound. Clanging of metal on metal. The burning sizzle of their weapon fire shooting electric bolts. The smell of burnt flesh. Cries of pain, surprise, and defiance.

It blends into a musical cacophony, the song of battle.

The lifting tide of it carries me. My opponents block, dodge, and weave around my attacks, but this only infuriates me.

When they land blows, the pain is fuel for the rage.

One falls before my onslaught. The other is falling back, I swing the lochaber up, around, the sound of it whistling in my ears when pain explodes thought and I'm falling.

The air is knocked out of my lungs as I slam onto the ground. Muscles won't respond. Muscles are spasming painfully. Contorting on the sand, I vie for control of my body. The scent of burning flesh fills my nostrils.

My opponent looms into view. His smile showing rows of sharpened teeth. His sword comes up. Get control, fight!

The dragon rages but my body refuses to respond, muscles are not under control.

The sword flashes, reflecting the double suns, slicing down, and all I can do is mentally brace myself for the pain....

A blur, and he's gone from sight.

The last of the spasms pass. As I gain control, I roll to one side coming to a stop on my knees. Ragnar wrestles with the Invader that was about to finish me. They roll over each other, struggling.

I scramble forward, grab my lost lochaber, and chase them down the side of the dune. They come to a stop and the Invader is on top, his sword at Ragnar's throat. The first trickle of blood drips down Ragnar's throat.

Swinging out, down, and then up, I take the Invader's

DRAGON'S REDEMPTION

head off in a drenching spray of blood. Ragnar throws the body off of himself and leaps to his feet, whirling on me wide-eyed. We stare at each other, primal instincts roaring, then the rage in his eyes clears and we nod.

I turn and run back up the dune to rejoin the battle. Ragnar comes up next to me and we survey the field.

"We have to stop those," he says pointing at the ones reaching the gate.

Two lone Zmaj guard the gate and they are fighting off a dozen Invaders. The odds are against them and they'll fall, sooner or later. Nodding my agreement we run forward in a desperate attempt to reach them in time. There seven Invaders between us and the dozen assaulting the gate directly.

We must win.

As I reach the closest of them, blocking his sword with my lochaber, something else catches my attention, distracting me.

Something slips out of the gate. A small body.

"Rag—"

I'm cut off by a fist slamming into my stomach. Air whooshes out, and I double over with the force of the blow. By twisting to the side, I dodge the sword driving down on the back of my neck.

He put all his force into the killing blow, following through with it, leaving him open. Ignoring my need for air, I move around his open side, wrapping my arm around his neck as I slide in behind him.

Squeezing hard with my good arm I shake him from side to side. If I had both arms, I'd be able to break his neck, but my injured arm hangs useless.

He grabs my arm, struggling, fighting to break free. Leaning back, pulling him tight against me, I swing my tail around and slam it repeatedly into his legs. Finally I hear the crunch I was hoping for, and I know that his legs are broken. He tries to scream, but I've cut off his air. He goes limp in my arms and I drop him.

"Move!" Ragnar yells.

He's standing over the body of another Invader. My vision of him swims, and for an instant he's a squad mate, the past overlays the present.

Binkaran, my friend. His face melts before my eyes as the blinding white light burns my retinas.

Shaking my head the vision clears and I'm here.

Ragnar. This is Ragnar.

Delilah. She's in danger. Focus.

Bounding into action, I follow Ragnar towards the gate, searching for what I saw a few moments ago. A small shadow. A high-pitched scream cuts through the uproar of battle.

"LET ME GO!" the little girl screams, struggling against the Invader crushing her to his chest.

The child. The one who greeted me so oddly. As if she knew me, had been waiting for me.

My feet sink into the sand as I run, leaping from one foot to the next, wings spread to take the air as I pick up speed.

Three Invaders are between me and the one holding her. Ragnar slams into one of them, and the other two form a defensive line, aiming guns in my direction.

No time. Can't fight them. The one holding the child is backing away, retreating. No one else is close enough.

I crouch down on landing and then I leap, pushing as hard as I can. Hot air glides past my face, as my wings catch the breeze.

The two Invaders are beneath me as I arc down. One I slam with my tail. The other brings his gun to bear, so awkwardly I slam the butt of my lochaber into his face. His nose crunches and blood spews.

DRAGON'S REDEMPTION

I lose air, dropping down, twisting to land with my feet on the shoulders of the one I hit with my tail, and I push off again and gain air racing toward the one with the child.

The child screams again.

"You're going to be in trouble!" she yells. "He's coming."

Does she know? How could she?

There isn't time to think it through. I'm losing air before reaching the one who has her, but I land behind him hard, sand bursting up to form a thin cloud. He hears or senses my presence, and he whips around to face me. He has a blade threatening the child.

His mouth moves and he chitters. Words. It doesn't matter what they are, whatever he says, he's dead. It's only a matter of time, because I'm going to kill him.

27

DELILAH

I can't keep up with Olivia. She's at a dead run, all but flying across the open area and heading for the gates. Samil tried to stop her leaving the cave but all he has managed to do is keep pace with her.

"Olivia," he yells at he again. "Stop, we'll take care of it."

"It's my daughter!" she screams, not slowing down.

The sounds of fighting drift through the partly open gate.

Partly open. It shouldn't be open at all. We're under attack. How in hell did Zoe do that? She's so small, she can't have opened the gate, can she?

Stupid. Such inane thoughts to be having when Zoe is in danger. Everyone else is in the cavern keeping the twins and the other babies from deciding to join the fray. I have to help Olivia, or stop her, or save Zoe.

I'm not sure which or what I'm going to do, but instinct demands I run with her. It's all I've got, and what I'm operating on right now.

Olivia slams against the partly open gate, exclaiming in pain or shock but the gate screeches open far enough for her to squeeze out of it, and I follow her.

174

My breath catches in my chest.

An Invader, blue-scarred skin almost black, four arms, armored and threatening as anything I've seen on Tajss is less than twenty feet away. The sight of him isn't what makes my blood run cold. It's what he's holding.

Zoe.

He has a blade held up close to her neck, but he doesn't even spare a glance in our direction. He's facing off with Jormund.

"You're in trouble!" Zoe yells, struggling in his grip.

"Zoe, hold still," Olivia says, her voice cracking.

"Zoe, it's okay," I say, stepping next to Olivia.

"I know," Zoe says, smiling at the two of us as if, for all the world, this is the most normal expected thing.

Jormund's wings spread and his tail rises straight up behind him as he leans into his stance, threatening the Invader.

"Delilah," he says. "Stay back."

He barely looks in my direction, but my heart gallops at the sight of him. He's strong, dominating my thoughts, even dominating the scene in front of us. He's so... *there.* So alpha, in control, and dangerous.

Dangerous.

That's the word that describes him best of all. My stomach clenches, mouth dries, palms sweat and I'm wet. So damn wet.

I want him. I need him. He's mine. My man, the male who will stand against the world and won't be beaten. I've never felt anything like I do right now. So much fear and desire, a storm of emotions that seem impossible to contain.

The Invader says something, but it's not words I understand. He takes a step back, keeping the threatening blade at Zoe's neck.

"Don't worry, Mommy," Zoe says. "It's all fine."

MIRANDA MARTIN

"Zoe," Olivia says.

"Mommy," Zoe says, exasperation in her voice, and she rolls her eyes at her mother. "Seriously, it's fine."

Olivia's mouth moves, but no sound comes out. She looks over, and I don't have an answer either, so I shrug. Zoe has always been special, seeming to know things that she couldn't possibly, but she does.

Her and Bashir, our resident seer, have had long walks together. We've all noticed it, whispered about it, but none of us know what to do or think with it so mostly we ignore it. But this… this is too much.

She's confident, certain, and it's obvious she at least thinks she knows what she's doing.

"It will be okay," I say, straining to get the words out past the lump in my throat.

"Oh God…" Olivia says, trailing off. Her hands flex and she shudders. "Baby…"

The Invader takes another stride back. Jormund watches him, like a cat watching its prey. On the ship I'd seen nature documentaries and that's what he seems like. A cat toying with a mouse. An alpha predator waiting for the moment it's going to tire of the game and act.

His eyes move with each motion the Invader makes, but his body is still, a rock, unperturbable. There's a sense of anticipation, building tension in the air. All of us feel it. The battles raging all around us continue, the sounds of steel on steel. Screeches of pain. War cries echoing off the stone of the wall.

None of it matters. All of that fades to the background. White noise against the scene before us. Olivia takes a step forward, unhooking one of the shock sticks from her belt and raising it aggressively. The Invader makes a quarter turn so that he's facing her too, bringing the knife closer to Zoe. He says something, it sounds like chittering.

DRAGON'S REDEMPTION

"No Mommy," Zoe says, still fearlessly calm. "That's not the way this goes. He has to save me. He belongs with us."

Ships engines drone loud as they whizz overhead. One of them comes to a stop, hovering above us. Suddenly it hits me, are they trying to get Zoe? Was that their target?

Why? How could that be?

It's insane. So crazy I don't dare say it, but could it be?

Suddenly Jormund moves. It's so fast I don't see him start. He's there, then he's not, and there's a blur. He leaps into the air, wings flapping, tail swinging behind him, the glinting steel edge of his lochaber held ready in front of him.

The Invader whirls, turning to face the threat. Time slows to a crawl. In slow motion, the blade closes with Zoe's neck. Her mouth opens, she leans her head back. Olivia moves forward, shock stick rising to attack.

The blade at Zoe's neck is close. Too close. I will myself forward, but time is a heavy weight holding each of us hostage. The space is too much. She's too far away. We won't make it in time.

Zoe kicks the Invader, struggling against his hold, then she's sliding down the front of him. Jormund whirls the blade around. The Invader raises the sword to block the attack.

The ringing of steel is followed by a cracking sound. The Invader's arm flops in an unnatural way that makes my stomach flop too.

Zoe runs for Olivia, leaping into her arms as Jormund finishes the Invader. Olivia whirls around with Zoe's head tucked into her chest, hiding the violence from her child the best she can.

And like that, it's over.

Time rushes, fresh air fills my lungs, my heart races, and I'm left shaking as the adrenaline drops out of my body.

The ship's engines whine louder and then rumble. The

ship above us darts away, followed by the others. The skies empty as the Zmaj walk towards us at the gates. In moments the males stand in a semi-circle, surveying the scene.

Jormund turns to face them. His injured arm, hanging limp at his side, drips blood onto the red sands. He grips his lochaber tight in the other hand, butt driven into the sand. I walk over to his side, in awe of his fighting prowess. In awe of *him*. He saved Zoe, single-handedly. It was incredible.

Drosdan steps forward from the semi-circle of males, coming to a stop a stride in front of Jormund. The two males stare at each other, silent. I don't dare breathe, afraid even the hint of my breath will be too much for the tension in the air. That its added weight would break the moment, send it spiraling out of control in a wrong direction.

A tremor runs through Jormund. I wouldn't notice it if I wasn't leaning against him. He has to be in pain, exhausted. We haven't slept, and he's been through beating after beating, but still he stands here, proud and defiant.

"I am myself," Drosdan says, his deep voice rumbling.

He doesn't say anything more. Expectation builds until I'm going to burst. Placing a hand on the small of Jormund's back I make small circles, offering what small comfort I can. Drosdan continues to wait. The males watch. No one moves, no one says more. What do they want? Obviously, there is some expectation here, but I don't know what it is, and no one is saying it!

"I... am... myself," Jormund says at last.

Drosdan nods.

"Together we are stronger," he says.

The silence falls again, and we wait. When I look up at Jormund, I see the light in his eyes. He's processing the words as if they resonate with something deep inside of him. He glances down and our eyes meet. I lose myself in his

DRAGON'S REDEMPTION

gorgeous eyes, swimming in the rich pools. The corners of his lips tug up then he returns his gaze to Drosdan.

"Together we are stronger," Jormund repeats.

Drosdan nods again.

"Survival of the group matters," he says.

Survival of," Jormund says no longer hesitating, his words coming smoother and somehow more natural, "the group matters."

Drosdan nods sharply then steps forward extending his left arm. Jormund takes the offered hand, clasping it at the wrist.

"Welcome, brother," Drosdan says, and cheers erupt from the watching males.

"I tried to tell you Mommy," Zoe whispers so soft I barely catch it.

When I glimpse her over my shoulder, she's all but beaming with pride. The rest of the males move forward, embracing Jormund, then as a group we go through the wall. I push them to hurry so I can tend to his wounds.

They've accepted him. He's part of the Tribe now. All my hopes and wishes have come true.

28

DELILAH

$\mathcal{H}$mmm. Maybe some more seasoning. I sprinkle some in and give the pot a stir.

"Smells delicious," Jormund says.

I smile, turning around to give Jormund a quick kiss. It's been a month since we came back to the Tribe and things have been great. More than great. They've been amazing.

After he saved Zoe in the fight with the Invaders, the other Zmaj accepted him, mostly. They watched him, sure, but he's a stranger. I wouldn't really expect less, but it didn't take long. People have gotten used to seeing him around the cave system now. He's well on the path to acceptance, forming bonds of his own.

"Do you need help?" he asks looking around.

His speech has smoothed out and become so natural you'd never guess that he didn't talk at all a few weeks ago.

"That would be great. Could you cut those up for me, please?" I ask pointing at the waiting vegetables.

He nods, taking a knife and getting to work. I prepare the meat I want to add to the stir fry.

"How was the hunt?" I ask as we work.

DRAGON'S REDEMPTION

"It was fruitful. Nobody was hurt, and we brought down two gusters."

I make an impressed noise. "Sounds very successful."

He nods, bringing the vegetables over.

"It is easier to take on larger prey with a group."

"That makes a lot of sense." I take the vegetables, setting them down next to the meat.

"Hmm." He wraps his arms around me from behind, nuzzling the side of my neck.

I smile, turning around in his arms.

"I have to finish dinner," I murmur, even as I wrap my arms around his neck.

"Everyone will be fine if it is late," he says, lifting me to make the fit easier.

His lips lightly touching mine. I melt into the kiss, sighing at the familiar feel of him against me. It feels new and like I've had him with me forever at the same time. Life is so good.

That edge of encroaching bitterness at not having someone of my own is gone. Not only that, I've gained a best friend, someone who loves all of me. I'm so damn lucky.

"Stop doing that near my dinner!" Ragnar barks, breaking our kiss.

I blush hard but luckily, it doesn't show on my skin tone. I'd never live it down if he knew he'd gotten to me.

"You're jealous," Jormund says, wrapping his fingers in my hair and forcing my head back so he can kiss me again. "I not tell you what do with your mate."

Jormund is grinning over the top of my head.

"I do what I do with my mate in our own private cave," Ragnar retorts. "Not near *food* others will eat! Get back to work!"

His words sound harsh but the humor in his voice is obvious. Looking over my shoulder to him I roll my eyes.

MIRANDA MARTIN

"If you want any food, you better speak in a softer tone," I threaten.

He holds his hands up in surrender with a childish grin on his face.

"Please?" he asks, looking sheepish.

I laugh, shaking my head as I slide down from Jormund. I dump the meat into the hot pan. If it was just Ragnar, I might have purposefully delayed dinner just to get back at him, but everyone will be waiting for the food, including the babies.

So Jormund and I finish up the rest of the food and bring it out to everyone within a half an hour.

"Thank God—I'm starving!" Penelope says, walking in to see the meal arrayed.

"Smells great Delilah! And Jormund!" Olivia says.

"I did little" Jormund responds, smiling.

We sit down at one of the large tables together, digging into the food. Dinner is a success. I smile, soaking in the compliments. It's nice to feel appreciated. And I really like to cook. In a lot of ways, this new life suits me better than my old one on the ship.

After dinner, everyone works together to clear away the dishes and then it's time for the nightly get-together. Instruments get tuned for the music and board games come out in full force, laughter and excited voices blending together to make a sound that I'll forever associate with home.

The people are what make a home, after all. The place is just the setting. Jormund and I take up station at a small bench, snuggling together to listen to the music. He starts to sing along in the deep baritone I heard the first time we gathered after dinner.

It's a gorgeous, warm tone that I could listen to forever. I look around at the gathered Tribe, the scene warmly lit, the crowd gathered in tight. Everyone is either smiling, laughing, talking, singing.

I turn my attention back to Jormund, who's looking down at me as he sings, a smile tugging the corners of his mouth. I smile back, leaning in to kiss his smiling mouth.

You know what? I can have it all. And now I do.

Thank God I was kidnapped.

THE END

ABOUT THE AUTHOR

USA Today Bestselling Author of fantasy and scifi romance, Miranda Martin's books feature larger than life heroes with out-of-this-world anatomy and smart heroines destined to save the world. As a little girl she would sneak off with her nose in a book, dreaming of magical realms. Today she brings those fantasies to life and adores every fan who chooses to live in them for a while.

She was born and raised in southern Virginia, but as a veteran she's traveled to places like Korea, Hawaii and good 'ole Texas. Now she's settled in Kansas, the heart of America, with her husband and daughters. Her favorite animals are dragons, unicorns and cats. If she's not writing, you can still find her tucked away somewhere with a warm blanket and her nose in a book.

Get in touch!
mirandamartinromance.com
miranda@mirandamartinromance.com

facebook.com/authormirandamartin
twitter.com/imMirandaMartin
instagram.com/imMirandaMartin

ALSO BY MIRANDA MARTIN

USA TODAY BESTSELLING AUTHOR

Red Planet Dragon's of Tajss Series
Red Planet Jungle Series
The Power of Twelve Series
The Alva Series
Dragon's & Phoenixes Series

Made in the USA
Monee, IL
30 April 2022

95663926R00114